The way Noah watched the parking lot, sweeping his gaze over the area, made Maddy nervous.

Surely he didn't think they'd be ambushed here? No, it was more likely that he was just being a cop.

The minutes ticked by with excruciating slowness, but then a large black K-9 SUV pulled into the parking lot, the twin headlights bright amid the dusky shadows.

Maddy headed for the door. Noah moved lightning-fast, grasping her arm, halting her progress.

"Hold on a minute, Maddy." He pushed her behind him. "I'm going first, just in case."

She didn't want Noah in harm's way, but he was wearing the vest that had saved his life once before. She grasped the back of his utility belt, determined to follow close on his heels.

Outside, her gaze centered on the black SUV she could see parked in a spot that was facing the bowling alley. The driver-side door opened and a man climbed out. Her brother turned and the moment she saw his face, the missing puzzle pieces clicked into place.

She let go of Noah and rushed around him in a hurry to reach her brother.

"Get down!" Noah shouted just before the boom of a gun echoed through the parking lot.

Laura Scott is a nurse by day and an author by night. She has always loved romance and read faith-based books by Grace Livingston Hill in her teenage years. She's thrilled to have published over twelve books for Love Inspired Suspense. She has two adult children and lives in Milwaukee, Wisconsin, with her husband of thirty years. Please visit Laura at laurascottbooks.com, as she loves to hear from her readers.

Books by Laura Scott

Love Inspired Suspense

Callahan Confidential

Shielding His Christmas Witness
The Only Witness
Christmas Amnesia

Classified K-9 Unit

Sheriff

SWAT: Top Cops

Wrongly Accused
Down to the Wire
Under the Lawman's Protection
Forgotten Memories
Holiday on the Run
Mirror Image

Visit the Author Profile page at Harlequin.com for more titles.

CHRISTMAS AMNESIA

LAURA SCOTT

H HARLEQUIN® LOVE INSPIRED® SUSPENSE

Recycling programs
for this product may
not exist in your area.

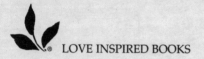

® LOVE INSPIRED BOOKS

ISBN-13: 978-0-373-45734-2

Christmas Amnesia

Copyright © 2017 by Laura Iding

www.Harlequin.com

Printed in U.S.A.

Answer me when I call to You, my righteous God.
Give me relief from my distress;
have mercy on me and hear my prayer.
—Psalms 4:1

This book is dedicated to my niece Brianna Umhoefer.
Always remember you are strong and smart.
Reach for your dreams!

ONE

Assistant district attorney Madison Callahan hesitated on the concrete steps of the Milwaukee County Courthouse, shivering in the cold breeze coming off Lake Michigan. Had she heard something? Or was she letting her imagination run wild?

Working late and leaving at nine o'clock at night wasn't unusual, but for some undefined reason she hesitated. Giving herself a mental shake, she continued down the stairs, careful to avoid any icy patches.

When she reached the bottom of the stairs, she instinctively headed toward the reassuring streetlight, digging in her purse for her phone. Normally she walked the three-quarters of a mile to her condo, but since the hour was late, she decided to pull up the ride-sharing app on her phone.

She was moments from confirming her pickup location for her ride when strong arms yanked her backward, causing her to drop the phone. She sucked in a breath to scream, but the arms tightened crushingly around her. The sharp edge of a blade pressed painfully against her throat.

"Drop the case or you will all die, including the two old ladies in the house on the hill."

Maddy froze, her mind grappling with what was happening. *Two old ladies* had to be referring to her mother and grandmother, but how did this guy know where her family lived?

She forced herself to speak. "Did Alexander Pietro send you?"

The blade pressed deeper, causing her to suck in a harsh breath from the sharp pain. Something warm trickled over her skin. Blood? Was this man going to slit her throat right here?

Headlights swept over the road, brightening as a vehicle approached, but before she could be relieved that help had arrived, the man holding her suddenly gave her a hard shove, causing her head to crack soundly against the solid steel of the light post.

Pain exploded in her temple and she felt herself falling, arms flailing as she sought to break her fall. Her last fleeting thought was that she needed to find a way to keep her mother and grandmother safe. If anything happened to them, she'd never be able to live with herself.

"Ma'am? Can you hear me?"

She moaned and blinked, the light overhead painfully bright. Her head was pounding so hard she thought she might throw up. "Yes," she croaked. "I can hear you."

"That's good." An older guy, with salt-and-pepper hair and thick black-rimmed glasses, filled her field of vision. He was blurry initially, but then became clear. "Can you tell me your name?"

"Huh?" Moving her head hurt too much, so she stared at the man. He was dressed in green scrubs, a stethoscope wrapped around his neck.

"Your name," he repeated patiently. "There wasn't any ID found at the scene."

She opened her mouth, then shut it again. Of course she knew her name. Didn't she? The pain in her head quadrupled and she winced, closing her eyes and swallowing hard, willing the contents of her stomach to stay put.

Panic gripped her throat, making it impossible to breathe. Why couldn't she tell this man her name? What was wrong? Could it be that the pain was making her confused?

Forcing her eyelids open, she stared at the stranger looming over her. Concern darkened his gaze.

"We need to get a CT scan of her brain," he said to someone nearby. "Make sure there isn't any intracranial bleeding."

If pain was a good way to judge potential bleeding, then she was all for the brain scan. But even as the hospital staff wheeled her over to the radiology department, she couldn't ignore the strange sense of urgency that weighed heavily on her chest. She needed to get up and out of here; there was something very important for her to do.

But what? There was nothing but a dark void where her sense of self should have been.

Not just her name, but all of her memories were missing, lost in the swirling vortex of black pain.

Thankfully the scan didn't take long. As she was being wheeled through the hallway back to the ER, at least what she assumed was an ER, a handsome man wearing a navy blue police uniform caught her gaze.

"Maddy? You're the mugging victim? What happened?"

She stared at him for a moment, hoping she'd recognize him. For some weird reason, the dark navy blue MPD uniform was reassuring.

Wait, MPD? Milwaukee Police Department? How did she know what the initials stood for? Why not Minneapolis or some other city?

No clue.

"Maddy," he said again, crossing over and reaching

for the side rail of her gurney. "What happened? Are you all right?"

It took her a long second to realize this man seemed to know her. "Maddy?" she echoed with a frown. "Is that my name?"

The officer's face paled with alarm and he kept pace with the orderlies who were currently pushing her through the hallway. "You don't know your name? Do you recognize me?" he asked.

"I'm sorry," she murmured, feeling as if she was letting this guy down. She hoped he wasn't her boyfriend or someone she'd once dated. He was attractive, with his short blond hair and deep brown eyes, and she could easily imagine herself dating a guy who looked like him. "My head hurts."

"Officer, you can't come into her room," the orderly said.

"Just try and stop me," the cop said, his features etched in a fierce scowl. "I'm here to take her statement."

"I'm getting Dr. Wagner." The orderly disappeared, leaving her alone with the officer.

"Who are you?" she asked.

"Noah Sinclair," he said, his gaze expectant as if the words would spark some sort of memory.

They didn't.

"You're with the Milwaukee Police Department, aren't you?" she asked.

"Yes. Maddy, I need to understand what happened. Who did this to you?"

"I don't know what happened." Boy, was she sick and tired of saying that! "All I know is that I woke up here, in the hospital with a skull-splitting headache."

"Listen, how about I call your brother? I'm sure once you see Matt, your memory will return."

Brother? It seemed wrong that she couldn't remember a brother. Although maybe she wasn't close to her family. For some reason she couldn't explain, she didn't want this cop calling anyone on her behalf.

"No. Please, don't." Reaching up, she managed to grasp his wrist, the warmth of his skin oddly reassuring. "I— Just give me a few minutes, okay? I'm sure I'll remember everything soon enough."

Officer Sinclair's deep brown eyes held indecision. She tightened her grip.

"Please. I need some time."

He glanced down at her hand on his arm, then lifted his gaze back to hers. "Okay, I'll hold off for now. But I hope that doctor comes back soon. I have a few questions."

"Thank you." Her hand slipped from his arm and she closed her eyes in an attempt to clear her mind. Her poor brain cells were scrambled like eggs. All she needed was a little rest.

She concentrated on breathing, in and out, allowing her muscles to relax. Someone, maybe the cop, turned the overhead lights off, leaving her alone.

Oh, that was much better. She had no idea if she normally did this type of relaxation technique, but it seemed to come automatically.

In and out. In and out. *Slow your breathing and your heart rate.*

Ignoring the vague sounds coming from the hospital staff, she concentrated on keeping her mind clear. Was it always this easy to think of nothing in particular?

She must have dozed a bit, because someone suddenly bellowed, "Hey! What are you doing in there?"

Prying her eyes open, she saw a deeply tanned man hovering close to her bedside. For a moment, his pale eyes held an angry malevolence, but then he turned away. "Cleaning," he muttered, pushing past the cop and the doctor and then hurrying away.

"Did he hurt you?" Noah demanded.

"No. He's just one of the cleaning staff."

"Maybe," Noah said in a low voice, his gaze following the tanned man as he made his way into another room. "I don't like it, though. I think it's best to get you out of here as soon as possible."

She looked up at Noah, searching her memory for anything that would help her remember. But there was only a vast emptiness. No name. No memory.

Nothing.

A horrible sense of helplessness tightened her chest. She'd asked for some time, but so far, that hadn't helped much. She still didn't remember anything. And then another terrifying thought hit her squarely in the gut.

What if her memory was gone forever?

Noah leveled the doctor with a hard stare. "Does she have bleeding in her brain or not?"

The ER doctor, Daniel Wagner, shook his head. "No, her scan was clear."

"Then I'd like to take her home." Noah had been upset to find out that Maddy Callahan had been mugged near the courthouse. But what was even more disturbing was that she didn't remember her own name. Or anything about her family.

The only thing working in his favor at the moment was that Maddy didn't remember him, either. Which meant she wasn't glaring at him or telling him to get lost in that lofty tone of hers.

Noah knew she blamed him for her brother Matt being stabbed in the stomach eighteen months ago. Matt and Maddy were twins, and truthfully she had a right to be angry. Noah had hesitated a fraction of a second too long, allowing the female drug addict to lunge at Matt, sticking the blade deep.

At least Matt hadn't been injured too badly; the tip of the knife had managed to miss his liver by a fraction of an inch. Matt claimed the assault wasn't Noah's fault, yet right after the injury, Matt had abruptly decided to pursue becoming a K-9 cop.

Noah knew the real reason was that Matt didn't trust him to be his partner any longer, and he couldn't shake the guilt that clung to him like a soggy woolen sweater. After all, Matt wouldn't have been hurt in the first place if Noah had reacted instantly to the threat.

Old news, he reminded himself. Time to get over it.

His radio went off, and he quickly turned away to answer it. His latest partner of just over six months, Jackson Dellis, was asking if he needed assistance to question the mugging victim. He assured the younger man he had it under control. Since their shift was officially over, he told his partner to go home and that he'd file the report on the mugging victim himself. Jackson didn't hesitate to agree.

Noah turned back to the doctor. "I'm a friend of the family and I'd like to take her home now," he repeated.

"Well…" The doctor hesitated, obviously not happy with the thought of letting his patient go. "She still seems to have some cognitive issues."

"More like amnesia, don't you think?" Noah countered. He crossed his arms over his chest. "Are you trying to tell me she has to stay in the hospital until her memory returns?"

"Not exactly," Wagner backtracked. "But she needs to be watched closely for worsening signs and symptoms."

Yeah, he could understand that. "Listen, Doc, I promise

I won't leave her alone. But since we don't know what happened to her, I think she needs to be taken someplace safe."

That made the doctor bristle. "Our hospital is safe," he protested.

Noah wasn't in the mood to argue. When he swept another gaze over the ER, he noticed the mop that the tanned guy had been using was lying on the floor as if it had been dropped and abandoned. The man himself was nowhere in sight.

Maybe he was being paranoid, but Noah couldn't help but think that Maddy's injury was related to the case she was scheduled to take to trial in less than a week.

Noah knew all about Alexander Pietro's drug-running business; he was one of the cops who'd helped arrest him. They had plenty of evidence, but Pietro had serious mob connections in Chicago, and Noah wouldn't put it past them to attempt to free Alexander by doing whatever was necessary.

Even threatening to take out the assistant district attorney handling the case.

The fact that Maddy was still wearing a pair of black slacks, topped with a dark gray blazer over a blue blouse that matched her eyes, confirmed that she'd been working late down at the courthouse.

"I'll check with my boss," Dr. Wagner said. He left Maddy's room and Noah remained where he was at the foot of her gurney. As far as he was concerned, no one was going to touch Maddy without his permission.

He glanced back at her, noticing once again the long slice along the front of her neck. A small portion of the scratch had been deep enough to require a few stitches. Imagining the way the mugger must have held a knife to her throat brought a flash of anger.

Nope. No one was going to touch Maddy Callahan again. No way, no how.

"Is there a problem?" A female physician entered the room. She was tall and beautiful with long curly red hair and it took him a minute to recognize her as Dr. Gabrielle Hawkins, the infamous trauma surgeon who'd saved the lives of numerous cops on the force. She was the best trauma surgeon on staff at Trinity Medical Center.

The prettiest one, too. Married, of course, to Deputy Shane Hawkins.

"Dr. Hawkins, I'm Officer Sinclair." Noah held out his hand and she gave it a firm shake. "This patient is Maddy—"

"Callahan," Dr. Hawkins finished, her eyes on the patient lying on the gurney. "I recognize her from when I took care of her brother Miles after he suffered a gunshot wound last April."

Noah figured he shouldn't have been surprised; rumor on the street was that Dr. Hawkins was exceptionally smart and never forgot a name or a face. "Yes. I have reason to believe she's in danger, so I'd like for her to be discharged into my care as soon as possible."

"Hmm." Dr. Hawkins skirted around him to approach Maddy. "Ms. Callahan? Can you open your eyes for me?"

Noah gripped the edge of the side rail as Maddy struggled to comply. Dr. Hawkins used a flashlight to examine Maddy's pupils and then had her follow a few basic commands. When she finished, she questioned Maddy about what she remembered.

"I don't remember anything," Maddy said, her brow deeply furrowed with obvious distress. "I don't understand, why can't I remember?"

Dr. Hawkins's smile was gentle. "It may be that you've suffered some sort of traumatic experience. I suspect that your memory will return on its own, but I'd like you to follow up in the neurology clinic in a week if the memory loss continues, okay?"

"All right," Maddy agreed and Noah knew then she really wasn't herself. The Madison Callahan he knew would never agree to a doctor's appointment in the middle of a trial.

Then it hit him. Until Maddy had her memory back, there wouldn't be a trial.

Oh, sure, maybe another ADA could pick up the case, but he knew from personal experience that getting ready for a trial took hours and hours of preparation. Maddy had grilled him about his testimony for a full eight-hour day and he was just one of the officers involved. What about the others? He couldn't imagine going through all that prep again.

Would the DA ask for a continuance? And if so, for how long? It wasn't as if they could just tell the judge to wait for Maddy's memory to return. Victims had a right to a speedy trial. What if they were forced to let Pietro out on bail?

The thought of Alexander Pietro being back on the street filled him with dread. Not just because the guy had threatened to kill every cop who'd participated in the bust, but more so because months of hard work would be lost forever. They'd have to start from scratch to build another case against him.

Placing more innocent lives at risk.

Noah curled his fingers into fists, knowing that he was taking the entire drug-trafficking case too personally. Because of his younger sister, Rose, who'd died of a heroin overdose when she was a senior in high school.

Another death that was mostly his fault. First Rose, then his former college girlfriend, Gina. One guilt piled on the other, with Matt's injury sitting at the top of the lopsided guilt cake.

He shook off the depressing thoughts and focused on the immediate issue at hand. Maddy hadn't wanted him to call Matt, but he'd called his former partner's cell number anyway. Matt didn't answer, so Noah left a vague message asking for a return call. Hopefully, Maddy's memory would return by the time Matt called back.

"I'll write the discharge order, Officer Sinclair, if you promise Maddy won't be left alone," Dr. Hawkins said.

"I promise I'll stay with her until someone from her family takes over."

Dr. Hawkins nodded. "Done. I'll have the nurse come in to explain what you should look for."

The nurse, a plump blonde with a cheerful smile, came into the room rattling off a list of signs and symptoms to be on the lookout for. Noah was glad when she handed him a packet of paperwork listing everything she'd just told him.

"Thanks," he said, folding the papers in half and sticking them in his back pocket. "Maddy? Do you need help sitting up?"

"I can do it," she said with a wince. She gripped the rail, pulling herself upright. She swayed, and he quickly moved closer and placed a steadying arm around her shoulders.

"Easy now," he said. "Take your time, there's no rush."

"I'm okay," she said, and the familiar stubborn edge to her voice made him smile. This was the Maddy Callahan he remembered.

The same woman Matt had warned him to stay away from the first time he'd laid eyes on her. Matt didn't want his baby sister, born a few minutes after him, to be in a relationship with a cop. The way Matt had lost his father, who'd happened to be the former chief of police as well as being murdered while visiting a crime scene, had made

Matt overly protective. Noah had completely understood where his former partner was coming from.

The warning hadn't been necessary since Noah had no intention of being in a relationship with anyone, especially not Madison Callahan.

Maddy swung her legs over the edge of the bed, placing her feet on the floor, then frowned at her stocking-covered toes. "Where are my shoes?"

"Here." Keeping a hand on her arm, he used his feet to bring the flats into position so she could slip them on.

"Thanks." She stood, then reached out to grab his arm. "Whoa. The room spins when I move too fast."

A flash of guilt assaulted him. Was he causing more harm than good by taking her out of here? Maybe he'd be better off asking for her to spend the night at the hospital so he could sit at her bedside, keeping an eye on her.

Then his eyes fell on the discarded mop. A tall man with thinning hair stood beside the mop, arguing with a middle-aged lady. There was still no sign of the man with the tanned skin, and the hairs on the back of his neck lifted in alarm.

No way did he believe the guy who'd been looming over Maddy was a hospital employee.

"Are you sure you're okay?" Noah asked. "I can probably convince Dr. Hawkins to admit you upstairs."

Maddy looked puzzled. "Who?"

"The red-haired doctor."

"You know her?" Maddy asked.

It was on the tip of his tongue to explain how she knew Dr. Hawkins, too, but he decided that would only make her feel bad. "Yeah, she's married to a cop, a deputy from the sheriff's department."

"Oh, I see. No, I don't want to stay here. I'd rather go

home." She frowned. "I must not have a purse or a phone, huh?"

"Unfortunately not. It appears the mugger took them." He bent over to grab her long coat off the chair. "Here, let me help you with this."

"Thank you." Maddy slid her arms into the sleeves as he held the coat for her. "Your mother must have taught you manners."

"Yeah." He didn't bother to elaborate since his mother had died a long time ago, and what was left of his family was scattered all over the globe. He and his siblings weren't at all close. In fact, he couldn't remember the last time he'd seen his older brother. Three years? Four? Rose's death six months after losing their mother to cancer had torn their family apart and, like the famous nursery rhyme, there hadn't been a way to put the pieces back together again.

He knew the Callahan clan was a tight-knit family and he wondered again why Matt hadn't returned his call. Should he start calling her other brothers? The only problem was that he didn't know their numbers and obviously Maddy couldn't help. Right now, she didn't realize she had five brothers—Marc, Miles, Mitch, Mike and Matt—every one of them older than her.

Wrapping his arm around Maddy's waist, he matched her slower pace as they made their way out of the emergency room. She stopped, looked surprised to see the Christmas tree in the lobby of the ER, as if she hadn't known the holiday was near. When they were outside, he gestured to a squad car in the small parking lot across the street. "That's our ride."

"Okay."

She ducked her head against the cold wind, walking alongside him down the sidewalk toward the parking lot.

As they reached the road, a car came out of nowhere, heading straight toward them.

"Look out!" Noah grabbed Maddy around the waist and leaped out of the way, landing in a snowbank on the other side of the road. The car came close enough to clip the back of his legs, then careened from view.

Noah stared at the retreating taillights, knowing that he wasn't imagining things. This was the second, maybe even the third, attempt on Maddy's life—if you considered that the tanned guy who'd been in Maddy's room wasn't a hospital employee—all in the span of a few hours.

All these incidents were related, he was convinced, to the upcoming trial of Alexander Pietro. And the thought of Maddy being in danger, not to mention having lost her memory, gave him a desperate sense of urgency.

Right now, he was the only one who could keep her safe.

TWO

"Are you okay?" The cop—she searched her memory; Noah?—helped her upright, brushing snow off her pants and coat.

"I don't understand. What's going on?" In the second she thought the car would hit her, she'd found herself praying for safety. Was that something she did on a regular basis? Must be, and for some reason, knowing that slight bit of information, that she believed in God and prayed often, helped calm her frayed nerves.

Thankfully Noah had reacted with lightning-fast reflexes, or she was sure she'd have ended up back in the ER with worse injuries. The hammering in her skull was bad enough, and it hadn't lessened one iota.

"You're in danger," Noah said in a grim tone. He put his arm around her waist, urging her toward the squad car. "I need to get you someplace safe."

"Why?" She braced herself with a hand on the squad car when he released her long enough to open the passenger-side door. "You think the mugging and this close call are somehow related?"

"Yes. I'll explain once we're somewhere safe," he said, his voice clipped.

She gingerly slid into the passenger seat. Noah shut the

door, then came around to climb in behind the wheel. She latched the seat belt, then rested her head back against the cushion and closed her eyes, swallowing hard against the increased pain.

Noah didn't break the silence, and she felt the car moving down the street. It wasn't until he took several turns, heading away from the hospital, that she opened her eyes and grabbed his arm, seized by a sense of panic. "Wait! I—I don't know where I live."

He flashed a reassuring smile, gently covering her hand with his for a long moment before letting go. "Don't worry, I do. You share a condo with a woman by the name of Gretchen Herald; she's a flight attendant for Airstream Airlines."

It seemed so wrong that this cop, this man, knew more about her than she did. Ignoring the pain in her head, she continued pressing him for information. "Tell me more, specifically why I'm in danger."

"Okay." His smile faded, his expression turning serious. "Maddy, you're an attorney, working in the DA's office."

His statement should have brought forth a flood of memories, but didn't. She stared at him, feeling stupid and not at all like a lawyer. "I am?"

"Yes. You have a big trial starting next week. A man by the name of Alexander Pietro is facing serious felony charges related to drug trafficking and gun running. Thanks to your impressive track record of winning guilty verdicts, you're the lead prosecutor on his case."

She stared at Noah's profile, straining to remember. Did the name Alexander Pietro sound familiar? Yes, it did, but she couldn't picture what he looked like. Was she remembering him from the case? Or because of something she'd heard about in the news?

Why couldn't she remember?

The deep sense of urgency returned with a vengeance. There was something important she needed to do. But what? The pain in her head intensified as she struggled to push past the haze in her mind.

"Don't, Maddy," Noah said in a low voice, reaching over to take her hand in his. "I don't think you should try so hard. Dr. Hawkins mentioned you need to rest, and relax. She believes your memory will return on its own."

"But when?" She couldn't help feeling as if she were standing on the precipice of a cliff, where one strong breeze would blow her over. "If what you're saying is right, that I'm working on a case, then I don't have time to wait around to see if my memory returns. I need to get back to work. Or call my boss, whoever that is, so he or she can assign someone else to the case." Then another thought hit her. "How do you know so much about this Alexander guy, anyway? Especially my involvement in the case?"

"I helped bring him down," Noah said, his tone matter-of-fact. He pulled up in front of a large brick building, gesturing to it. "I don't know if your roommate is home or not. Since your purse is gone, I'm assuming you don't have your keys."

Instinctively, she patted her coat pockets, surprised when she felt the distinct bulge. "I do have keys," she said, pulling them out of her right-hand pocket with a frown. "That's odd. I wonder why they weren't in my purse. Isn't that where I usually carry them?"

"I don't know, but right now I'm glad they weren't." Noah took them from her fingers. "That makes things easier for us, especially if your roommate isn't home."

She stared at the building, searching for something, anything that looked familiar. There were a few Christmas decorations in some of the windows, but overall, the place looked impersonal, as if it could contain anything from offices to apartments, no different than any other building they'd passed along the way. Of course, it wasn't easy to see clearly in the darkness. She couldn't imagine living there, yet Noah had no reason to lie to her, either. Was she crazy to trust him, just because he knew her and her brother?

Who else could she trust?

"Are you ready?" he asked.

She ignored the sense of dread. "Of course."

"Give me a minute," Noah said. She couldn't help but be impressed when he came around to open her door. Why was she so impressed with Noah? Was it possible the men she dated didn't have these kinds of manners? "Here, take my hand."

"Thank you." His hand was warm and strong around hers, and she was struck again by how handsome he was. It was inappropriate to focus on something like that, considering she didn't remember her own name, but still, she couldn't deny she was grateful for his strong, reassuring presence.

The inside of the building was very modern and nicely decorated, but didn't look at all familiar. Noah pushed the button on the elevator, and the doors instantly slid open. There were six floors and apparently she lived right in the middle on the third level.

She followed Noah down the hall to room 304. There weren't many doors, indicating the dwellings were spacious in size rather than piled one on top of the other.

"Stay here," he said, using her key to access the condo. He pushed open the door and flipped on the lights, looking around before gesturing for her to come inside.

She crossed the threshold, hoping, praying that the holes in her memory would begin to fill in enough to create a picture she could latch on to. But while the inside of the condo was nice and neat, it still didn't seem familiar. And worse, it didn't instill a sense of home.

There was a tiny Christmas tree in the corner, but it wasn't lit up. A detail that also seemed wrong, somehow.

"You're sure this is where I live?"

"You and Gretchen," Noah said. "Although I'm assuming that since the doors to both bedrooms are open, Gretchen must be traveling. If I remember correctly when I helped you guys move in, you have the room on the right, Gretchen's is on the left."

Swallowing a pang of disappointment, she walked around the living room, searching for what? She had no idea. There was a laptop case on the counter, so she crossed over and peeked inside. The computer didn't look familiar, but then again, why would it? Nothing personal about a machine. There was a paper file folder inside labeled Pietro. Hmm, that was interesting. Something to review in more detail later.

She turned away, searching for something personal. She headed toward the bedroom off to the right, thinking that she probably had family photographs since Noah had mentioned a brother. She'd only taken two steps when the soft dinging sound of the elevator door reached her ears.

"Wait," Noah said in a hushed tone, plastering himself up against the wall near the door, quickly twisting the dead bolt into place and shutting off the lights. "Get down."

When she saw the gun in his hand, Madison ducked behind the kitchen counter, her heart thudding painfully in her chest. He doused the lights, and for several long minutes they waited, the silence thick and oppressing.

The door handle rattled as someone tried to gain entry. Maddy found herself holding her breath, wondering if this was her roommate returning home from a late flight. But then she quickly dismissed the idea, knowing a roommate would simply use her key, the same way she and Noah had.

Another rattle of the doorknob caused the tiny hairs on the back of her neck to rise. Someone was trying to access the apartment.

To get to her?

More jiggling noises—what could the person in the hallway be doing? Picking the lock? She wished she could see Noah's face.

After what seemed like a lifetime, the noise stopped. She didn't move, waiting for some sort of signal from Noah.

The minutes passed slowly. When her leg muscles began to cramp from crouching, Noah came over to stand beside her, resting his hand on her shoulder. "Are you all right?" he whispered.

No, she wasn't all right. She couldn't remember anything about her past, her job, her life—plus someone had tried to hurt her not just once, but twice. She swallowed hard and pushed past the wave of anxiety. "Yes."

"We can't stay here," Noah continued in a hushed voice. "Whoever was out there might come back, or worse, hide someplace nearby to watch the place. I need to take you far away from here, someplace no one will know to look for you."

Her condo wasn't safe. The idea was terrifying, but then again, everything seemed surreal, as if this was happening to someone else, not her. Was that because she couldn't remember her past?

"Okay," she agreed, because really, what else could she say? She wasn't in a position to argue. She had no idea where to go or who to turn to for help.

Only Noah Sinclair, her buoy in a rough sea.

"Is that your computer case?" Noah asked.

"I think so. There's a file labeled Pietro inside. Although it's odd that it would be here when I was supposedly working late. Wouldn't I carry my computer with me?"

"I don't know. You could have been doing prep work with a witness. Regardless, let's take it with us," Noah said, releasing her to snag the strap of the case off the counter. He swung it over his shoulder, then reached for her hand. The moonlight shining in through the windows provided enough illumination for her to see his dark frame now that her eyes had adjusted to the darkness. "Come on, we'll need to take the back staircase down to the first floor."

She wanted to ask how he knew about the back staircase, then realized he'd mentioned helping her move in. Ironic that he knew more about the place she lived in than she did. In fact, it was clear Noah knew everything about her, which once again made her wonder about their relationship. Were they friends? Something more? Had they dated at one point? Sneaking another glance at his handsome profile, she thought that if he'd asked her out, she'd have said yes.

Then again, maybe she already had a boyfriend. There were no rings on her fingers, which made her feel slightly better about being attracted to Noah.

Enough. Stay on track, she admonished herself. Her headache must be making her loopy. There were more serious issues facing her right now than wondering about her personal relationships or lack thereof. "Can I pack a suitcase?"

"No time. We need to get out of here right away." His hand tightened around hers.

"Okay." She closed her eyes for a moment, sending up a prayer for safety, before following Noah to the door. He cracked it open, peering in the hallway to make sure the coast was clear.

"Let's go." He slid through the opening, using his broad shoulders as a shield in front of her as they made their way to the exit sign at the end of the hallway.

The stairwell was brightly lit, causing her to screen her eyes with her hand, wincing at the pain ricocheting through her skull. She followed Noah down the stairs, trying to mimic his soft, stealthy movements.

The way he paused at each floor, opening the doorway and looking down the hallway as if searching for anything out of place, caused her muscles to knot with tension. What if the door-handle rattler came back and found them?

She trusted in Noah's ability to protect them, but the thought of him putting his life on the line bothered her.

And as they made their way to ground level, Maddy couldn't help but wonder if she'd ever feel safe again.

The stark fear in Maddy's blue eyes made Noah grit his teeth against a surge of anger. This wasn't right. Maddy was a lawyer doing her job; she didn't deserve to be stalked by Pietro's goons.

Yeah, there was the remote possibility that it was someone else who held a grudge against the assistant district attorney. Maddy had assisted in putting other criminals away. Rumor had it she was one of the up-and-coming ADAs with an impressive conviction rate. Yet the timing of the assault against her was suspicious. Noah firmly believed that Alexander Pietro was the mastermind behind these recent attempts on Maddy's life.

Pietro had the most to lose. Maddy was the ADA standing in the way of his ability to beat the charges against him. The idea that Pietro might actually succeed in getting away with his crimes was unbearable.

For a second, his younger sister Rose's face flashed in Noah's mind. He remembered the way he'd last seen her—

pale and lifeless, lying on the floor of her bathroom, with a needle and syringe still embedded in her skinny arm.

Dead from a heroin overdose.

Then there had been Gina, the girlfriend he'd broken up with because of her relentless partying. She'd later died from alcohol poisoning.

He stopped so abruptly that Maddy bumped into him from behind. He automatically reached out to steady her. "Sorry."

"What's wrong?"

The way she gazed up at him, as if she actually cared about how he was feeling, made him cringe. He felt like a fraud. If Maddy's memory was intact, there's no way she'd be here with him right now. In fact, she'd likely demand Noah stay far away from her.

But she didn't have her memory and the danger surrounding her was all too real. He told himself to focus on the immediate threat. They were on the ground floor and unfortunately, he had left his squad car on the street directly in front of the building.

Smart, Sinclair. If the guy inside the apartment building was the same one who tried to run her over, he knows you're here. Idiot!

Too late to do anything about that decision now. He eased the door leading outside open a bit, looking out to be sure that no one was waiting there for them.

He didn't see anyone, but hesitated, unwilling to make another mistake, especially with another Callahan's life hanging in the balance.

If anything happened to Maddy, her twin brother, Matt, would never forgive him.

Noah wouldn't be able to forgive himself, either.

"What are we waiting for?" Maddy whispered.

Good question. Was he overreacting? Maybe the person outside Maddy's door wasn't trying to hurt her at all, but simply had the wrong apartment.

Then again, that wasn't a risk he was willing to take. He could call for backup, too, but he didn't like the idea of anyone with a police scanner knowing where they were. For all he knew, the guys working for Pietro could be listening in. "Stay behind me. I need to be sure that the coast is clear before we return to the squad car."

He could feel Maddy's fingers grabbing on to his belt and her simple trust had him deepening his resolve to protect her no matter what. "Whatever you say," she whispered.

The icy wind greeted him as he pushed the door open. Moving outside, he stayed close to the wall, grateful they were both wearing dark clothing that would help them blend into the night. He swept his gaze over the area, seeing nothing out of place as Maddy let the door close softly behind her.

They were on the south side of the building, and the street where he'd left his squad car was in the front facing west, so he edged closer to the back side of the building.

There was a narrow alley there, the darkness impenetrable. Noah considered their options. They could circle the building, making sure it was clear before making a run for the squad car. Or they could leave the car, making their way on foot until they could flag a taxi or car service for a ride.

He'd rather have his own set of wheels. While taxi and service drivers needed to pass criminal background checks, he knew the checks weren't foolproof. Decision made, he crept through the narrow alley between buildings until he reached the north side of the condo.

Peeking around the corner, he still didn't see anything

out of place. Feeling better, he made his way up to the street where he'd left his vehicle.

"Ready?" he asked, glancing over his shoulder at Maddy.

"Yes."

"Here's the plan. I want you to stay behind me. I'll protect you until you're safely inside the car."

"I don't think—" she began, but he shook his head.

"Not open for discussion. I'm wearing a vest beneath my uniform."

"Fine." She didn't look happy but kept her hand on his belt. "Let's go."

Noah held his weapon ready as he cleared the corner of the building. The squad car wasn't as far away as he'd anticipated, so it didn't take long to reach the passenger door. Yanking it open, he swept his gaze over the area as Maddy ducked into the passenger seat. He shut the door, then quickly jogged around to the driver side.

He jammed his gun into the holster and then cranked the key, bringing the engine roaring to life. Pulling away from the curb, he made a quick right-hand turn and headed east toward the lakefront.

"We made it," Maddy said softly.

He didn't say anything, keeping a keen eye on the rearview mirror for a possible tail. The hour was approaching one thirty in the morning and he was grateful traffic was light this time on a Monday night.

"Thank you, Noah."

He wanted to tell Maddy not to thank him, that if she knew who he was and how many people he'd let down, she'd never thank him for anything ever again, but he held back. For one thing, her memory loss was hardly her fault. And for another, it was easier to keep her safe when she was cooperating with him.

Headlights flashed behind him, the high beams blindingly bright. He was on Lake Drive now, following the shoreline of Lake Michigan, when the headlights grew closer and impossibly brighter.

"Who is that?" Maddy asked, grabbing for the door handle as Noah took the curve faster than the speed limit recommended.

"Hang on," he warned, pressing the accelerator.

There was a loud bang as the car behind them rammed into the back of his squad car. Noah wrestled with the steering wheel, straining to keep the car on the road.

He reached for his radio to call for backup when the car rear-ended them again.

This time, his police cruiser skidded sideways off the road, heading straight for the icy waters of Lake Michigan.

He hit the brakes, but the car didn't slow down. He tried again, desperate to avoid the freezing cold lake. If they went under, they'd surely die.

THREE

"No!" Maddy screamed as Noah yanked on the steering wheel, doing his best to keep the car from going into the water. They spun, but then hit something hard, bringing the vehicle to a stop.

She was thankful Noah had gotten things under control, but then the vehicle abruptly tipped backward, the rear tires dropping over the edge of the embankment lining the shore. There was a hiss as something hot, maybe the muffler, sizzled, the back end of the car sliding into the freezing cold water.

She fumbled with her seat belt, the car teetering precariously on the ledge. She knew that if she and Noah ended up in the lake, they risked severe hypothermia and possible death.

"Maddy!" Noah must have already unlatched his seat belt, reaching over to help her. "Hurry! We have to get out of here."

"I know." The hood of the car was raised up at an angle, the back end submerged. She gasped in alarm as the car slid backward another inch. No doubt the trunk was filling with water, and she had no idea how much longer they had before the rest of the vehicle would sink silently beneath the inky surface.

Hurry! Hurry!

The restraint fell free and Noah grabbed the computer case that was nestled between her feet. He looped the case over his shoulder, accidentally knocking the police radio off his collar in the process. Using both hands, he pushed open the driver-side door, then reached down to grab the radio before jumping out of the car.

"This way," he said, keeping his arm wedged beneath the heavy door. Maddy climbed over the console, sucking in a harsh breath when she cracked her elbow against the computer mounted on the dash. The space from the floor of the car to the ground was farther than she anticipated.

She lightly jumped down, but the uneven terrain caused her to stumble against Noah. He caught her up against him, holding her close and preventing her from hitting the ground. But she accidentally hit the radio draped over his arm, sending it down into a pile of slush. She knew water and electronics were a bad combination and Noah must have agreed because he didn't bother attempting to retrieve it.

Headlights pierced the night, pointing directly at them. She averted her gaze from the blinding glare, searching for someplace to hide.

"Hold on to me," Noah said, keeping his arm anchored around her. "See the rows and rows of boats stored up on blocks? That's where we're going."

She didn't answer, concentrating on following his lead as they quickly ran, slipping and sliding over to the closest row of boats.

The sound of a car door slamming shut caused her heart to leap into her throat and she imagined the driver of the car was already running after them. She clung to Noah, grateful for his support as she struggled to keep up. The boats were large and provided some cover from the bright headlights, but not enough that they wouldn't be seen.

Fear tightened around her throat. Did Noah believe they could outrun the guy behind them? Maybe if he was alone, but she knew her being here was an added liability.

If only she was wearing her running shoes.

Did she have running shoes?

This wasn't the time to worry about her lost memory. With the threat before them, the throbbing in her temple had lessened a bit, and she tried to ignore it. Pushing the ridiculous thoughts from her mind, she focused on following Noah as he moved from one boat to the next. He seemed to be checking them out, for what she had no idea. Plastic shrink-wrap covered most of the boats, protecting them from the harsh winter weather.

When they reached the middle of the sea of boats, Noah stopped. She leaned against a fiberglass frame, using the opportunity to catch her breath. Noah was doing something with the boat next to her, unlatching bungee cords holding a tarp in place, rather than the usual shrink-wrap. Peering through the darkness, she could see that two of the boats had tarps in lieu of plastic, and Noah worked on both of them.

She hoped he didn't plan on using one of them as a hiding place. Considering most of the boats were covered, it wouldn't take a genius to figure out that they'd take refuge in one of the two boats not shrink-wrapped in plastic.

Straining to listen, she attempted to pinpoint where the guy following them might be located. For a long moment she heard nothing but the gentle lapping of the waves against the shore. She was about to whisper to Noah that they should keep going when she heard the distinct sound of a muffled thump.

Noah froze, turning toward her. She stared at him, wondering if the noise was from the guy on their tail or from the squad car falling the rest of the way into the lake.

She reached for Noah's hand, needing his reassuring strength. As if he knew what she was thinking, he pulled her close and lowered his head so that his mouth was next to her ear. "We're going to be okay."

The tightness around her chest eased, enabling her to take a deep breath. Noah gently tugged on her hand, indicating they needed to keep moving. When she passed the two boats he'd been fiddling with, she realized he'd unlatched several of the cords holding the tarp, leaving a slight gaping hole.

Why on earth? Then it occurred to her that Noah had done that to make it look as if they'd chosen to hide inside the empty boat. If the attacker believed they were inside, he might waste time searching for them inside the boats.

Good thing she was on the run with a smart cop. One she trusted to keep her safe, no matter how steeply adversity was stacked against them.

Dear Lord, thank You for bringing Noah Sinclair into my life when I needed him the most. Please continue guiding us and keeping us safe in Your care. Amen.

The whispered prayer formed in her mind without conscious thought and she immediately felt a sense of peace and hope wash over her.

Noah was right; they would be okay.

When they reached the edge of the boat storage area, she tightened her grip on Noah's hand. Now what? This area of the marina was brightly lit, without offering many places to hide.

Surprisingly there was a boat still in the water, anchored to the pier. It looked as if the motor was running. The water around the engine was swirling. There was no sign of the boat's owner, but that didn't mean he—or she—wasn't nearby.

But they didn't have time to waste searching, either.

"See that boat?" Noah asked in a hushed tone. "That's our target."

She resisted when he tugged her forward. "We can't," she hissed. "That's stealing!"

"Borrowing," Noah corrected. He pulled his cell phone from his breast pocket, showing it to her. "I'll call it in as soon as we're safe."

She didn't like it, but then again, allowing the guy on their heels to capture them wasn't a good option, either. "Okay, let's go."

Leaving the shadows to step into the light took a tremendous amount of courage. She hunched her shoulders, trying to make herself a smaller target as they approached the dock. Walking along the pier was just as treacherous, the moisture from the lake mixing with the snow to create a slick surface. She walked as fast as she dared, following Noah as he approached the boat.

She glanced around, expecting the owner to be somewhere close by. Why else would the motor be running? Then again, the guy could be on the boat, too.

The lapping waves caused the boat to rock against the buoy in a rhythmic pattern. Noah braced his palms on the edge of the boat, really more of a small yacht, and used the flashlight on his phone to peer inside.

"Hurry," he urged, gesturing for her to come over. Maddy swallowed a wave of apprehension, putting her trust and her faith in Noah.

"You first," he whispered. After slipping his phone back into his shirt pocket, he held the boat steady while assisting her aboard.

The rocking motion caused her to stumble, and she accidentally yanked on Noah's hand, tugging him forward. She widened her stance, trying to find her balance. The fact that her head still ached didn't help, although pain was the least of her worries.

Noah leaped into the boat, then leaned over to unleash the ties. The boat immediately drifted away from the pier, so she hurried over to assist. Her arms weren't long enough, so she could only watch helplessly as he stretched out to unhook the second tether.

Leaning over the way he was, she shouldn't have been surprised when his phone slipped from his pocket and landed in the lake with a soft *ker-plop*.

She closed her eyes against a stabbing frustration but there wasn't time to worry about the submerged device now. The boat was loose in the water, so Noah quickly disappeared inside the pilothouse to take control.

The sound of the engines revving to life seemed incredibly loud, giving away their location to anyone within a hundred yards. She stumbled inside the pilothouse mere seconds before she heard someone shouting at them to stop, followed by the sharp retort of gunfire ripping through the night.

Noah hit the throttle, sending the boat surging out from the marina into the large lake, praying for the first time in years that none of the bullets would hit the vessel.

"I can't believe he's shooting at us," Maddy said, coming up to stand beside him. The enclosure of the pilothouse helped keep the stiff breeze away, but the cold December air still surrounded them.

"Don't worry, he can't follow us." Noah divided his gaze between the buoys on the water and the boat's navigation system. He hadn't sailed on Lake Michigan in four years, but basic geography made it impossible to get lost. If he hugged the shoreline, he could head south all the way to Chicago or go due east to Michigan.

Heading north would take them toward Green Bay, but he didn't want to go that far. He turned the boat south. His partner, Jackson Dellis, lived near the border between Milwaukee and Racine, and he was fairly certain there was a smaller marina in that area, too.

"Is there a radio on this boat?" Maddy, so cold that her teeth were chattering, asked. "We need to call for help."

"There is, but I don't want to alert the Coast Guard," he said. "I'd rather find a way to contact my partner."

"Wh-why not the C-Coast Guard?"

Noah glanced over at Maddy, knowing he should have done a better job of protecting her. Dr. Hawkins had ordered rest and relaxation, and the past few hours had been anything but. At this rate, her memory might never return.

"Because right now I don't want the entire world to know that you're suffering from amnesia," he explained. "Alexander Pietro is going to be tried by a jury of his peers starting next week, but we know he still has a lot of guys working for him. We need to make sure nothing related to your situation leaks into the press."

"Police reports are open to the public," Maddy said, her expression thoughtful.

"Yeah. Of course, the Milwaukee Police Department can limit the information that gets out, but your name has been linked to Pietro's case a lot already. Even the merest hint of an attack on you will have the media swarming all over it. I think it's better for now that we keep this quiet."

Until your memory returns, he added silently, refusing to consider the possibility that it might be lost long enough to derail the trial.

No way. He couldn't bear the thought of Pietro getting away with his crimes.

"And your partner will stand by your decision?" Maddy asked with a frown.

"I hope so." Jackson was his third partner in the last eighteen months, and so far he seemed okay. At least the younger guy hadn't dropped any hints about needing a partner that would back him up, the way his previous partner had. Matt hadn't held him responsible for the stabbing, but other cops hadn't been shy about sharing their opinions, especially Lynda. When Jackson had replaced her as Noah's new partner, Noah had been secretly relieved. Yet if he were honest, he didn't know Jackson Dellis very well yet. He couldn't say for sure if he'd agree with Noah's decision to keep the series of incidents surrounding Maddy quiet.

He didn't plan on giving him an option. Jackson was only in his second year of being a cop, so Noah would pull rank if he had to.

"I hope so, too," Maddy agreed. She shivered and moved closer. He put his arm around her in an attempt to share his warmth. "How are we going to get in touch with him without a phone?"

Good question. It was already past two thirty in the morning; even those places that catered to the nighttime crowd would close down soon, if they hadn't already. "I'm not sure," he admitted. "We'll think of something."

Maddy fell silent and he wondered if she was second-guessing her decision to go along with him. It hadn't been an easy last few hours for her. Although he hated to think about what might have happened if she'd gone off on her own. From the near miss outside the hospital, to being rammed off the road toward the icy lake, to being shot at as they sped away on a borrowed boat, the bad guys, no doubt hired by Pietro, had remained one step behind them.

Too close for comfort.

Noah cranked the wheel of the boat into a sharp right, toward the much smaller and not as brightly lit Racine Marina. When they were a nautical mile away, he pulled back the throttle so that they drifted quietly toward the pier. Sweeping his gaze over the area, he didn't see anyone lurking around, but he refused to relax his guard.

"I need you to hold the wheel steady," he instructed Maddy. "Then when I give the signal, put the engine in Reverse, see here? Just enough to prevent us from ramming into the dock, okay?"

"No problem." She placed her small hands near his, taking over the wheel the way he'd showed her. Fighting the instinct to hold her close, Noah moved away and headed out to the deck. He grasped the edge of the pier and quickly looped one of the boat's mooring lines over it.

"Now," he said and she instantly pulled the lever down, sending the engine into Reverse. "Off," he said, as he quickly secured the second rope. She turned off the key, and he waited for her to come over to join him.

"Ready?" He helped her step off the boat onto the pier first, then came up behind her.

"What's next?" Maddy's voice sounded weak, betraying her exhaustion.

The area was far more deserted; only a few boats were stored here for the winter. He spied an old building off to the left. "This way." He headed in that direction, relieved to see that the place was a snack bar used during the sailing season. It was boarded up for the winter.

Banking on the fact that there would be a phone inside, he examined the door. It was locked up tight and the windows were covered, as well. Refusing to give up, he checked every bit of plywood, finding one that wasn't secured as tightly as the others.

"Are you breaking in?" Maddy asked, sounding horrified.

"We need access to a phone."

"Even if there is a phone inside, that doesn't mean it will work," Maddy argued, sounding so much like her old self that it made him smile. "If they were smart, they'd shut down the phone line over winter."

"Yeah, but there's a chance they didn't bother. The sailing season extends beyond just the summer months."

"I—I guess it's worth a sh-shot." Her teeth were chattering again and Noah hoped that his instincts were right. Prying the plywood away, he managed to reveal a broken window.

Using his leather jacket–clad elbow, he knocked the rest of the glass out of the way and then poked his head inside. There were boxes stored beneath a counter, and thankfully a phone hung on the wall near the door.

"I'll be right back." He didn't like leaving Maddy alone, but this wouldn't take long. He handed her the computer case for the time being, then levered himself up through the window. It wasn't easy—his shoulders were stuck momentarily—but then he was inside. Lifting the phone receiver, he closed his eyes with gratitude when he heard a dial tone.

He punched in Jackson's number. The ringing seemed to go on forever and just when he was afraid he wouldn't answer, he picked up.

"H'lo?" His partner's voice was slurred with sleep.

"Jackson? It's Noah. I need your help."

"Noah?" Now he sounded more awake. "Do you realize it's almost three o'clock in the morning?"

"I know, I'm sorry, but I'm in a jam. Can you meet me down at the Racine Marina?"

"Now? Seriously? Is it important?"

"Yes."

Long silence, then, "Yeah, okay. Give me fifteen minutes."

"Thank you." He replaced the receiver then checked the door. A giant padlock hung through the latch, so he gave up and crawled back out the window. Maddy was huddled against the building, her arms crossed and her chin ducked into the collar of her coat.

After taking the computer case from her, he didn't hesitate to gather her into his arms. "Jackson will be here soon. I need you to hang in there for a little while longer, okay?"

"I—I can't get warm," she whispered.

"I know." He rubbed his hands up and down her back, hoping to ward off the possibility of hypothermia. She had a winter coat on, but no hat or gloves or decent boots. No wonder she was shivering. He tucked her head into his shoulder and tried not to be distracted by the cinnamon scent of her hair.

If Matt knew what a terrible job Noah was doing in protecting Maddy, he'd be furious. Which made him wonder why Matt hadn't called him back. The only thing he could imagine that would keep Matt from returning his call was if he was out on a case. Of course now that his phone was in the bottom of the lake, it didn't matter much.

He should have mentioned Maddy being in danger; then for sure nothing would have stopped Matt from returning his call. But back when he'd made that initial contact, he hadn't realized just how serious Maddy's situation was.

For a moment, Noah debated going back inside the building to make another call to Matt, but decided against it. He didn't want to leave Maddy alone and Jackson would be here soon. He could easily borrow his partner's phone to make the call. This time, Noah would be sure to give

Matt the specifics on how many attempts had been made on Maddy's life.

"Headlights," Maddy whispered, her body going tense, her breath warm against his throat.

"I'm sure it's Jackson," he assured her. They stood in the shadow of the building, a spot that provided them a broad view of the parking lot while keeping them hidden. He knew his partner drove a large pickup, so he waited until the vehicle pulled into a parking space to make sure. Yep, the truck looked familiar, so he felt certain Jackson was the one behind the wheel.

Sure enough, the driver-side door sprung open, revealing a short redheaded guy. Jackson climbed out and stood for a moment, glancing around expectantly, his expression irritated that Noah wasn't anywhere in sight.

He released Maddy and tried to step away, but she tightened her grip. "No, wait. I don't like this."

"That's my partner," he reminded her. "I'm sure we'll be fine."

"Noah, please…" Her voice trailed off.

"We don't have another option," he told her. "We need to get someplace warm."

She hesitated for a moment, then capitulated. "All right."

Before they could step out from the shadows, there was a loud crack and Jackson Dellis crumpled to the ground in a heap.

Noah sucked in a harsh breath, horrified to see his partner shot before his eyes, thinking, *Not again, not again!* But then he focused on protecting Maddy, dragging her deeper into the shadows, trying to comprehend what had happened.

Their only escape route had been effectively cut off, leaving them stranded at the mercy of a hidden shooter.

FOUR

"Stay down," Noah said, pushing her behind him. Maddy huddled close to his back, holding on to his utility belt, shivering at the realization they were vulnerable here, near the back edge of the building.

She'd known something was off, but hadn't expected this.

Another shot rang out and the truck's windshield shattered into millions of pieces. Noah's partner didn't move, but there was a large pool of blood on the ground around him and she suspected the poor guy was dead.

Maddy's heart was lodged in her throat. "We need to get out of here," she whispered. She knew it wouldn't take the gunman long to figure out they were hiding in the shadows of the small structure. "We don't know where the threat is coming from."

For several long moments, he didn't say anything. "I believe the gunman is up on the hill." Noah's soft voice held a steady calmness she envied. "Let's stay here in the shadows for a moment."

She drew her coat up over her face and twisted around to look up at the snow-covered hill looming above the parking lot. Her stomach knotted, because if Noah was right, they had to assume that being up so high gave the gunman the advantage. He would see them if they left their hiding place to run toward the boat.

But what choice did they have? For all they knew, the gunman wasn't alone. He could sit up there picking them off while sending someone else down to find them.

"Okay, here's the plan," Noah whispered. "The minute I return fire, we run for the boat. I want you to use a zig-zag pattern while trying to stay directly in front of me so I can protect you."

Maddy didn't like leaving Noah exposed, but nodded, trying to take comfort in the fact he was wearing a bulletproof vest. "Okay."

"If anything happens to me, I want you to keep going for the boat. Use the radio and call the Coast Guard and insist on being connected with either Miles or Matthew Callahan. They're both cops with the MPD. Don't talk to anyone else until one of your brothers shows up. Understand?"

Two brothers? He'd mentioned one earlier at the hospital, but two? And they were both cops? Somehow, that part didn't surprise her. Maybe that was why she'd subconsciously recognized Noah's uniform.

"All right," she whispered. "But here's the deal. I don't want anything to happen to you, either. We're both going to get out of this alive, understand?"

Noah flashed a grim smile, then waited for another long moment, the night air eerily silent. Maddy wanted so badly to leave this place, wishing they'd never come here. Or that they'd called Noah's partner here. What if the gunman was making his way toward them right now?

She wrestled the panic under control, sending up a silent prayer for assistance.

Dear Lord, protect us from harm!

The boom from Noah's gun was so unexpectedly loud, her ears rang and the pounding headache intensified. But she didn't let that stop her. Instantly, she whirled and ran around the corner of the structure. Moving as fast as she dared, she ran across the open space, heading toward the boat bobbing up and down in the water.

She could feel Noah behind her. Knowing he was placing his life on the line to protect her made her run faster. Gunfire rang out behind them and she swallowed a sob, jutting one way, then the other in an attempt to make it more difficult for the gunman to hit them.

"Oomph," Noah muttered.

"Are you hit?" She wanted to turn around to see what was wrong.

"I'm fine, keep going," he whispered.

The pier was growing closer. She juked left, then abruptly turned right. Ten yards. Five. She pushed for more speed, leaping onto the pier and then diving into the boat.

Thankfully Noah was right behind her, stopping long enough to remove the lines keeping them connected to the dock. Without waiting for him to tell her, she went to the pilothouse and started up the engine.

"Go!" Noah shouted, jumping into the bow of the boat just as another round of gunfire echoed through the night.

She didn't need to be told twice. Hoping she didn't wreck the boat engine doing something she shouldn't, she pulled the throttle into Reverse. The boat shot away from the shoreline, rocking dangerously on the water.

Praying the bullets wouldn't render the boat useless, she did her best to get control so she could command the boat farther out into the center of the lake. A few minutes later, Noah came over to join her.

"We need to go farther south," he said, reaching around her to turn the wheel, pointing the boat southeast.

"What if the gunman follows?" she asked, grateful they'd managed to escape.

Noah kept his hands on the wheel, his arms bracketing her on both sides, and she was comforted by his strong, reassuring presence. "Don't worry, we'll stay far enough from shore that they'll soon lose sight of us."

She hoped he was right. Turning her head, she looked up at him. His face was set in grim lines. "Are you sure you're all right?"

He didn't answer right away, and she belatedly realized he was grieving over his partner.

"I'm sorry about your partner," she said softly. "We need to call the authorities, send them to the Racine Marina. Maybe he's still alive."

Noah shook his head. "He was hit in the chest and went down like a rock. I doubt he was wearing his vest. I should have warned him…" His voice trailed off.

She covered his hand on the wheel with hers. "You didn't know there was a gunman hiding on the hill."

Noah didn't respond and she could tell that he was beating himself up over his partner's death.

"If this is anyone's fault, it's mine," she tried again. "The only reason you called him is because you were stuck protecting me. I'm the real target here, right? This Pietro guy is after me."

He glanced down at her, and she wondered if it was just her imagination or if there was a softness in his expression now. "Yes, but trust me, Pietro would love nothing more than to kill me, too. In fact, there's a chance he's put a price on the head of anyone who helped get him arrested."

Maddy swallowed hard, trying not to show her horror. It was bad enough that she and Noah were in immediate danger from this man, but knowing there might be other targets he was going after made it much, much worse.

She needed her memory to return. Before more innocent lives were lost.

* * *

Noah ignored the pain spreading throughout the right side of his back. As long as he could move, he wasn't going to waste time stopping to inspect the damage.

The vest he was wearing had saved his life, and Maddy's, too.

But not Jackson's. The image of his partner threatened to send him to his knees and guilt choked him.

When would the deaths stop?

The boat lurched to the side, and he realized he'd loosened his grip on the wheel. This wasn't the time to feel sorry for himself. He needed to stay focused, to clear his thoughts. To find a way to keep Maddy safe.

Nothing would bring his partner back. All he could do was keep moving forward. Find a way to bring Pietro's henchman, if that's who was behind all this, which was the only thing that made sense, to justice.

But his partner's unexpected shooting begged the question about how the gunman had found them in the first place? Had Jackson's phone been bugged? Or had his partner been followed to the marina? If the guy who'd rammed them into the lake was working for Pietro and had figured out Noah's name, it stood to reason that they'd assume he'd go to Jackson for help. The gunman might have staked out Jackson's place and when he figured out they were headed for the marina, went over to pick his spot on the hill.

Was it possible someone from within law enforcement was involved? As soon as the idea entered Noah's head, he pushed it away.

No, he wasn't going there. Besides, he had no evidence that these attempts against Maddy were the result of an inside job.

Maddy settled back against him. He told himself not to read into her gesture; she was likely freezing cold and seeking warmth. Even if she one day decided to forgive him for causing her twin brother's injury, there would never be anything but friendship between them.

He didn't do relationships. Losing his sister and then Gina had taught him that love hurt. He wasn't about to open himself up to that again, and especially not with Matt's twin sister. She was off-limits in every way.

The cinnamon scent of her hair was distracting and he kept his eyes on the water, making sure there weren't any vehicles that seemed to be tailing them.

Should he turn around and head back to Milwaukee?

He considered the cities and towns north of Milwaukee. There were a few areas that would serve as a good hiding place.

But there was the temperature to consider. Maddy had already been exposed to the elements for too long. Dr. Hawkins had told him she needed rest and relaxation. The sooner he could find them a safe place to spend what was left of the night, the better.

Heading north was out of the question, so he focused on finding a place that was within walking distance of the southern shore of the lakefront.

Easier said than done.

Maddy shivered, accentuating the need to get her someplace safe and warm. He eyed the fuel gauge. Was there enough to take them to Chicago? Then again, maybe just getting across the Illinois border would help.

Five minutes passed, then ten. He was beginning to give up hope of finding anything close by when he caught a glimpse of a neon sign.

Vacancy.

Perfect. But where was the motel? Objects in the distance could look deceiving. What appeared close was likely farther away than he'd like.

He cranked the wheel, pointing the bow of their boat toward shore. The vacancy sign grew brighter and he was relieved to see that the small structure was adjacent to what looked like a truck stop.

Sweeping his gaze over the area, he stumbled across a small boathouse next to a pier. It looked private, but he didn't care. They needed safe access to shore, and from there he would let the boat drift away, hopefully taking anyone working for Pietro far away from their hiding spot.

Maddy didn't say anything as he steered the boat toward shore. In fact, she took over the wheel, leaving him to guide the vessel to the pier, as if they'd done this together a hundred times, instead of just once.

"Now," he called. The engine immediately went into Reverse and he looped the line over the pylon. "Cut the engine."

She did. Within seconds, she joined him in the bow.

"Take my hand," he instructed, hiding a wince when his back muscles screamed in protest.

Maddy stumbled, her movements sluggish, and he knew hypothermia was beginning to set in. They didn't have any time to waste. He needed to get her inside the warmth of a building as soon as possible.

"Come on, Maddy, we're almost there," he urged, taking more of her weight so that he could get her onto solid ground. When she was standing on the pier beside him, he quickly lifted the line off the pylon and gave the boat a firm shove with his foot.

"Wh-what are y-you doing?" He took it as a good sign that her teeth were chattering again. At least her body was still attempting to stay warm.

He needed her to fight for just a little longer.

"If Pietro's men are watching, they'll hopefully assume we're still on board." He wrapped his arm around her waist. "The motel isn't far, see the vacancy sign? Warmth is just a few yards away."

"I—I see—it."

Was it his imagination or were her words coming slower and more slurred? He urged her forward, anxious to get to their destination. Dividing his attention between Maddy's precarious health and searching for signs of danger, he took the shortest possible route to the motel.

The lobby of the motel was dark except for a small lamp he could see at the front desk. As they approached, he didn't see anyone standing there and when he tested the door, it was locked.

Since the truck stop café was open and likely serving coffee, he gestured to it. "We'll stop in there, get something hot to drink."

This time she didn't respond and it appeared she was having a hard time putting one foot in front of the other. The light shining from the café was like a beacon.

After what seemed like forever, but was less than a few minutes, they reached the building. He opened the door and practically shoved Maddy inside. When the door closed behind him, the interior warmth hit him like a welcoming embrace. He found himself closing his eyes and praying.

Thank You, Lord, for giving me the strength to get Maddy to safety.

As they dropped into the closest open booth, it struck him that praying for Maddy was instinctive and much easier than praying for himself.

Maddy cradled the mug of hot chocolate in her hands, taking tiny sips to warm her belly. She hadn't realized just how cold she'd been until she'd stumbled into the warmth of the café.

She glanced over at Noah, who was sitting beside her,

rather than across the table. Maybe it was her imagination but she thought she could feel warmth radiating from his hand that was resting on her knee.

Shivers racked her body, which made it difficult to drink the chocolate. In some tiny corner of her mind, she understood how dangerously close she'd been to succumbing to hypothermia.

"Thank you, Noah," she whispered.

He stiffened. "You shouldn't be thanking me," he said in a flat tone.

"Yes, I should. Without your help, I'm fairly certain I'd already be dead," she said, knowing she owed her life to this man, this officer who'd put his own life on the line to protect her. "I wish I remembered—well, everything, but especially you. I'm sure we were friends before this."

Noah shrugged. "Friends might be pushing it. We were acquaintances, nothing more." He cleared his throat, obviously uncomfortable with the topic. "Since we're here, we may as well order breakfast. When the motel opens up, we'll grab a room."

She couldn't bear to let go of the steaming mug long enough to open the menu, so she rested her cheek against Noah's shoulder and looked at his. "I'll have a veggie omelet and a side of hash browns."

A wry grin tugged at the corner of his mouth. "You still don't eat much meat, do you?"

That observation made her frown. Had she ordered the veggies because of a buried memory? And if so, were there other memories that might begin surfacing? She sincerely hoped so. "I guess not," she said. "Is there anything else you know about me? You mentioned two brothers, earlier. Do I have parents, too?"

Their server chose that moment to approach their table,

refilling Noah's coffee mug and asking if they were ready to order.

Noah ordered a sausage-and-mushroom omelet rather than the veggie, but they both requested hash-brown potatoes as their side. After the woman hustled away, he turned to look at Maddy, his deep brown eyes, the color of melted chocolate, serious.

"You have a large family, Maddy. Five brothers, a mother and grandmother. Your father was killed in the line of duty almost two years ago. If you want me to call your brothers, I will. I don't like the idea of using an unsecured phone in the motel, but if that's what you want, we'll find a way to make it work."

A large family? Her breath caught in her chest. How was it that she'd completely forgotten everyone in her family? A mother? Brothers? Grandmother? It didn't make any sense.

Thinking made her head ache. "I don't know what to do," she confessed softly. Logically it would make sense for Noah to call her brothers, handing her over into their care, but the idea of leaving him to go off with men she didn't know wasn't appealing. Granted, he'd been a stranger at first, but now she felt comfortable with him.

Scary how much she'd come to depend on Noah.

"Listen, let's eat, get some sleep and see how you feel in a few hours," he suggested. "It's still pretty early. No reason to raise the alarm right now, and maybe by then your memory will have returned."

She nodded, trying to ignore the lingering headache. "That sounds good to me. I'd rather not risk anything happening to my family, the way—" She stopped just short of mentioning his partner.

Noah's expression turned grim. "Then we're in agreement," he said. He gently squeezed her knee, then removed his hand. She immediately missed the warmth of his touch.

The food arrived with surprising speed. Maddy bowed her head and murmured a quick prayer before digging into her breakfast. By the time they'd finished their respective meals, and a second hot chocolate, Maddy noticed the main lights had been turned on at the motel across the street.

She'd finally stopped shivering, and she didn't relish the thought of heading back out into the biting cold, even for a short trip across the road. Yet sitting in the booth made her realize how exhausted she was. Her eyelids drooped and she wished she could lean again on Noah.

"Ready?" Noah asked, as she drained the last of her second hot chocolate. He'd paid the server in cash, leaving a nice tip.

"Sure." She forced a smile.

He slid out of the booth first, then offered her his hand. She took it, glancing up at his face as he helped her stand. A flash of pain darkened his eyes, making her frown.

"Are you sure you're okay?" she asked. From what she could tell, he wasn't bleeding anywhere.

"Of course." He didn't say anything more, and she shrugged it off, thinking her tired mind was playing tricks on her.

He opened the café door for her and she sucked in a harsh breath as the biting cold hit her face. Instantly the shivers returned.

"I'm here, and we'll be inside again soon," Noah said, wrapping his arm around her waist.

She nodded and fixated her gaze on the single light in the lobby and the loops of garland hanging around the window. Within moments they were inside, sheltered from the icy wind.

Noah requested two adjoining rooms and used his badge to convince the manager to allow him to pay in cash.

The rooms were nothing fancy, but clean. Noah knocked on their connecting door, so she went over to unlock her side.

"I know you need privacy, but humor me by leaving your side unlocked and ajar, okay? Just in case."

After everything that had transpired over the last several hours, she knew his request was more than reasonable. "Of course."

"Get some rest," he said with a gentle smile.

"You, too." She left her door open an inch, then quickly washed up in the bathroom. When she returned, she heard a muffled groan from next door.

"Noah?" She pushed open the connecting door. Noah was wearing a white T-shirt and was bending over to pick up the bulletproof vest from the floor.

"It's nothing," he said, but the paleness of his skin and the beads of sweat gathering at his temples belied his words.

She crossed over and took the vest from his hands, running her fingers over the surface. The gear was heavier than she'd expected and it didn't take but a moment to find the bullet lodged three inches to the right of center.

She felt her own color draining from her face at the evidence she was staring at with her own eyes. A bullet. Smashed beyond recognition embedded in the material. Noah had almost died tonight, protecting her. If he hadn't been wearing his vest...

The consequences were unthinkable. She barely knew Noah Sinclair, didn't remember anything about him, or her own history, but at this moment she couldn't imagine her life without him.

FIVE

Noah mentally berated himself for being loud enough to draw Maddy's attention. Unfortunately, bending over had caused a sharp pain to lance through him, which meant he may have cracked a rib or two.

He reminded himself that Maddy had been injured, too, worse than he had. So he sucked it up. "I'm fine, Maddy, the vest did its job."

She tossed the vest over the back of a chair. "You're bruised, though, aren't you? I know that the force of a slug still packs a punch, in spite of wearing protective gear."

Bits of her memory were coming back to her, which both gave him hope and filled him with dread. He forced himself to focus on the former. Maddy needed her memory in order to try the case against Pietro; his personal feelings didn't matter.

"Yes, but I'll survive. It's not the first time I've been hit."

Her blue eyes widened in horror. "It's not?"

Oh, boy, that was the wrong thing to say. He tried again. "I'll be okay. The bruises will fade in a few days. Please try to get some rest."

She stared at him for so long, he had to fight not to squirm beneath the intensity of her gaze. "You should take some ibuprofen for your back," she said. "There's a convenience store adjacent to the gas station. I'm sure they have some."

"That's a good idea," he said, even though he had no intention of leaving her alone. "They'll have toiletries and other items there, too. Get some rest and we'll check it out, later."

She frowned and crossed her arms over her chest, tilting her chin defiantly. "You need the ibuprofen now, Noah. I'm not leaving until you go out to get it."

The familiar Maddy stubbornness made him smile. She was so tired she was practically swaying on her feet, but he also knew that she wouldn't budge until she got her way. He considered taking her with him, then decided he could be there and back in a matter of minutes. Faster, really, than if he dragged her along.

"I'll go if you stretch out and relax. Deal?"

"Deal."

He dragged his jacket back on and crossed over to head outside. Walking swiftly and ignoring the pain, he purchased the ibuprofen along with two toothbrushes, toothpaste, a hairbrush and two warm fleece sweatshirts, one for each of them. If she was going to insist he shop, then he'd make sure to take care of her needs, as well.

When he returned to his room, he was relieved to see that Maddy had indeed stretched out on her bed and was already fast asleep.

Moving silently, he set the personal items he'd purchased for her on the dresser in clear view for when she woke up, before returning to his room. He downed the ibuprofen, and then sat on the edge of his bed. The computer case caught his eye, and it occurred to him that he might be able to find a picture of Maddy's brothers to show her when she woke up. It was something productive he could do now, since he wasn't about to risk using the motel phone.

Jackson's dead body flashed in his memory, and he closed his eyes, willing the image away.

There was nothing he could do about his partner; right now, his priority had to be keeping Maddy safe. Which meant helping her to recover her memory as they stayed hidden.

Shoving his exhaustion aside, he pulled out the computer and turned it on. He silently groaned when he discovered the device was password protected.

Of course Maddy would be sure not to leave her work unsecured. He considered guessing her password, but didn't want to risk locking it up for good.

He turned off the computer and turned his attention to the manila file labeled Pietro.

He carried the folder over to the bed and stretched out with the pillows propped against his sore back. The ibuprofen barely took the edge off, but he hadn't expected it would help much anyway.

But a hot shower might. He rolled off the bed and headed into the bathroom. When he emerged twenty minutes later, the soreness in his back muscles had loosened up.

He dressed in his uniform pants and the sweatshirt, then began reviewing Maddy's file. Maybe there was something in there, some detail that would help him uncover a clue as to who might be working on Pietro's behalf.

It didn't take long for the words to swim on the page. The next thing Noah knew, he was blinking at bright sunlight shining in through the window.

The clock on the bedside table read eleven thirty in the morning. He'd slept for almost five hours, and while his brain felt clearer as a result of his nap, the muscles in his back had grown stiff from lying in one place for so long.

Swallowing a groan, he awkwardly rolled into a sitting position. There were muffled sounds coming from Maddy's room, indicating she was up, too.

Sure enough, in less than a minute she knocked lightly on his side of the connecting door. "Noah?"

"Come in," he said, making an effort to hide the level of discomfort he was feeling.

She entered his room, looking adorable in the navy blue sweatshirt he'd purchased for her. "How's your back?"

"Sore. How's your memory?" He thought for sure it would have returned by now.

"Still vacant, like a wide-open empty field." Her gaze zeroed in on the Pietro file with the precision of a laser beam. "What are you doing? You can't read that." She came over, scooping up the papers and shoving them back into the file. "What were you thinking? You're a key witness for the prosecution—reviewing my notes jeopardizes my case!"

"I guess your legal memory is back," he said. Her scowl deepened and he raised a hand in defense. "Relax, I don't remember reading anything before I conked out. I haven't compromised your case, I promise."

"You better not," she warned, hugging the file close to her chest. "If—*when* my memory returns, I'll have a lot of catching up to do."

He rose to his feet and crossed over to Maddy. "I had a thought about how to spur your memory to return." He gestured toward the computer. "You might have photos of your family on there, but it's password protected so I can't get in."

She stared at the device. "I'm not sure I know my password, either," she admitted softly.

"It's worth a try," he said, injecting confidence in his tone. "Your memory about what you like to eat and about your job seems clear enough. Maybe you'll instinctively remember."

"Maybe." Her tone lacked certainty. She dropped into the chair next to the desk, set the Pietro file aside and turned on the computer. Resting her fingers on the keys, she appeared to wait for some deeply rooted instinct to kick in.

After a few seconds, her hands dropped to her sides and she slowly shook her head. "I don't know. *I can't remember!*"

He immediately regretted putting her on the spot. "Hey, it's okay. It's not important. I'll call your brother Matt, okay? I'm sure when you see him, your memory will return."

"No!" She twisted in the chair to glare at him. "I don't think that's a good idea. I don't want to place my family in danger."

Her words were something that he could easily imagine her brothers saying. Being protective of their family was truly a Callahan trait. So different from what his family was like. "Maddy, listen." He pulled up a second chair and sat beside her, taking her hands in his. "You need to trust me. Matt is a good cop. I won't tell him where we are, but I'll suggest a meeting place, somewhere public with a lot of people around. He'll want to be there for you."

"But Jackson— You said yourself, whoever is after me knows who we are. They must have tapped Jackson's phone. How else would they have known he was coming to help us?"

There was nothing wrong with her ability to perform deductive reasoning, that was for sure. Noah was impressed that she'd made the connection.

"And that means they know my family, too. I refuse to put any one of them in danger."

"Maddy, we need help. We can't do this alone, especially since your memory hasn't returned yet. We need disposable phones, additional clothing and a vehicle. I don't have enough cash, and we can't afford to leave an electronic trail."

"But…" Her voice trailed off and soon he could see resigned acceptance in her eyes. "I wish we could use a pay phone, instead of the one here at the motel."

"I didn't see one at the convenience store, or the diner, either. But the best way to keep Matt safe is to provide a meeting place in a populated area. I doubt the gunman who followed Jackson to the Racine Marina would have taken so many shots if it had been daytime in a crowded place."

She closed her eyes for a moment. "You don't know that for sure. If he was well hidden and had an escape route planned, he may have taken the chance."

Realizing there wasn't anything he could say to ease her mind, he let it go. No point in making rash promises he might not be able to keep.

"Go ahead and make the call." She pulled her hands out of his, and rose to her feet, as if needing to put distance between them. Guilt, his familiar companion, rested heavy on his shoulders.

What else could he do to ensure Matt's safety?

The woman at the front desk. He could offer some money to use her cell phone. It wasn't foolproof, personal cell phones could still be traced, but it would take longer. Possibly giving them the head start they needed. "I'll be right back," he said, reaching for his coat.

"Why? Where are you going?"

He briefly explained his plan, then rushed back out in the cold air. The sun was up, but the temperature surely wasn't. Ducking his head against the icy wind, he walked to the lobby.

The woman behind the desk looked to be in her mid-fifties and he hoped she'd be sympathetic to his cause. The lobby was also empty, so there wouldn't be anyone listening in.

"Ma'am, would you be so kind as to allow me to borrow your personal cell phone?" He set his badge on the counter along with a ten-dollar bill. "I need to make a long-distance call and I can't use the phone in my room."

She looked at him with suspicion, but then shrugged and scooped up the ten-dollar bill. "Why not?" She pulled the phone out of her purse and entered her pass code. "Stay where I can see you, sonny. No funny stuff."

"Yes, ma'am." Noah quickly entered Matthew's phone number—thankfully he'd memorized it from their time together as partners—and listened to the ringing on the other end of the line.

After ten long rings, Matt's voice mail came on. Noah turned a bit so that his back was to the woman at the desk, and spoke in a low, urgent tone. "Matt, it's Noah. Maddy is in extreme danger related to a case she's working on, and we really need your help. It's vitally important that you meet us this afternoon at four o'clock at the Rosemont bowling alley. Please finish up whatever you're doing to meet us there. We'll be waiting for you."

He disconnected from the line and then deleted Matthew's number from the phone's memory so the woman couldn't see what number he'd called before handing the device back to her. "Thank you very much."

She checked the phone, seemingly disconcerted by the lack of evidence related to the call. "You're welcome, officer."

Should he try Miles Callahan? He didn't know Matt's older brother very well and didn't know his personal phone number, either. He could try to get the information from dispatch but there was no guarantee they'd give it to him. Since Maddy was closest to her twin, he decided to leave it alone. If for some reason Matt didn't show, then he'd have no choice but to move on to plan B.

As he returned to the motel room, he hoped and prayed he and Maddy wouldn't need a plan B. Noah had purposefully used four o'clock in the afternoon, not just because that was when darkness began to fall, but also to give Matt plenty of time to finish up whatever he was doing to meet them. He couldn't imagine Matt not rushing to his twin sister's aid.

Unless he was physically hurt, or worse. A remote possibility he had no intention of relaying to Maddy.

She'd suffered enough already.

Maddy shoved the computer out of the way to make room for the Pietro file. Her lack of memory was starting to make her mad, and it occurred to her that reviewing the details of the high-profile case she must have lived and breathed for weeks on end might help.

To her dismay, the notes didn't feel at all familiar. Panic tightened her chest and she forced herself to slow her breathing. In and out. In and out.

She focused on reading the entire report she'd included in the file. The names didn't help spur any recognition, but she pushed on.

The door opened, bringing a rush of cold air as Noah returned. She glanced over. "Did you talk to my brother?"

He grimaced and shook his head. "No, but I left a message. I'm sure he'll meet up with us at four o'clock this afternoon at the Rosemont bowling alley."

The place didn't sound familiar, either. "Noah, maybe you should take me to my office. I'm sure someone there will restore my memory."

"I'm not sure about that. Besides, returning to your office is too dangerous. Not just related to your personal safety, but what if your memory doesn't return? People will greet you and expect you to know who they are. No, the risk of your amnesia leaking to the press is too great."

He had a good point. She gestured to the file. "There's nothing in here about Pietro's known associates. I must have that information on my computer."

Noah shrugged off his jacket, then came over to sit beside her, his woodsy scent a soothing balm on her ragged nerves. She thought again how fortunate she was to have him there, protecting her.

"Let's try to figure out your password," Noah said. "You're closest to your brother Matt, so try a combination of your names."

She tried MadMatt and a few other variations without success. "Wait, what's my birthday?"

"April 4," Noah said. "Same as Matt's, you're twins. Matt was born a full three minutes before you."

Twins? No wonder they were close. Maddy tried more variations of their names along with their date of birth. Then she typed in *Twins44ever* and instantly the computer screen opened, revealing a beautiful landscape of fall leaves in full color.

"Autumn is your favorite season," Noah said.

She smiled weakly. Once again, Noah knew more about her than she did. Clicking on the file explorer, she was stunned to discover she had several documents listed under the name of Alexander Pietro.

"Wow. This must include everything I have related to the case," she said, overwhelmed by the amount of information she possessed. She was about to open one of the files, but then hesitated, glancing at Noah. "Maybe you should let me look through this on my own first."

"Maddy, if your memory doesn't return, there may not be a trial," he said with clear exasperation. "I think finding the man who's trying to kill you takes priority over your worry about me seeing something I shouldn't."

She minimized the screen, but remembered the date in the lower right-hand corner. "Today is Tuesday, right? It's only been a little over fourteen hours since I lost my memory. If I can get it back later today or tomorrow morning, then there's still a chance I can bring the case to trial. Putting Pietro behind bars for the rest of his life is my top priority. Finding the accomplices working for him has to be secondary."

"Not if they find you first," he argued.

She swallowed against a lump of fear. It was unacceptable to allow Pietro to scare her away. She lightly grasped Noah's arm. "Please, Noah. Just give me a little time alone to review the files."

His dark brown eyes clung to hers, then dropped to her hand, pale against the tanned skin of his forearm where he'd shoved the sweatshirt sleeves out of the way. His arm was warm and strong.

"Fine." Noah abruptly shot to his feet and she let him go, feeling the anger radiating off him. "But I don't think keeping me out of the investigation is the best way to get this case to trial."

She hated to admit he might be right. Still, the need to keep the integrity of her case intact overrode all else. Noah crossed over and turned the TV on to a local news station and she took her computer back to her room, doing her best to ignore him.

She clicked on a document labeled "Pietro's known associates." When the file opened, she noted that she'd neatly listed names followed by whatever information she'd uncovered about them.

Unfortunately, the names didn't mean anything to her. She could have been reading a recipe for cabbage soup, instead of identifying someone who might have come after them.

Not just once, but several times; killing Jackson, and shooting Noah in the back.

Remembering the slug she'd found in his vest made her shiver. Noah had placed his life on the line for her, over and over again. She stared at the list of names.

It was no use. She needed Noah's help with this. He'd been a part of the team who'd arrested Pietro, so it was possible that he knew many of these known associates already.

"Noah? Would you mind taking a look at this?"

The television went silent and he came through the connecting doorway to lean over her shoulder, peering at the screen. He whistled softly between his teeth. "That's some list you have there."

"Does anything jump out at you?" she pressed. "I'm sure you know some of them, but you may not know them all. I need to know if anyone from this list jogs your memory."

He was so close she could feel the warmth of his breath against her hair. The woodsy scent was stronger now, and she had an insane urge to throw herself into his arms.

"This one," he said, reaching around her to tap gently on the screen. "Lance Arvani."

Her pulse quickened and not just because of Noah's nearness. "What about him?"

"He was in my class at the police academy. We graduated together, seven years ago. Are you sure he's a known associate of Pietro? Last I heard, he was working for the Chicago Police Department."

No, at the moment she wasn't sure about anything. She

stared at the name, wondering how or why she'd connected Arvani to Pietro. Why hadn't she left additional notes?

Was it possible that this was the link they were looking for? Noah thought it was likely the shooter at the marina had ties to the police, but this? A cop who was still active on the force?

She tightened her fingers into fists, battling a wave of helplessness.

Why couldn't she remember?

SIX

Noah stared at Lance Arvani's name, trying not to be distracted by Maddy's nearness. He hadn't liked Arvani much; the guy had come across as arrogant and in-your-face.

But not liking a guy was a far cry from accusing him of being involved with a known drug trafficker like Pietro.

"You don't remember seeing him at all during the drug bust?" Maddy asked.

He straightened and shook his head. "No, and I'm sure I would have recognized him if he was around." He gestured to the computer. "Do you mind if I do a little searching for information on him?"

She didn't hesitate to turn the computer so he could access the keyboard from the chair beside her. "I'd love to see a picture of him."

"That part is easy." He found their academy graduation picture. Lance was on the opposite side of where he'd stood, and the image of his own serious yet youthful face made him wince. His father hadn't come to the ceremony, and neither had any of his siblings. Noah remembered standing there, thinking about how he was going to work hard to make the city a safer place, so that kids like his sister Rose wouldn't have such easy access to drugs.

He'd been naive, really, to think that one person could have much of an impact.

"Oh, look how handsome you are!" Maddy tapped her finger on his picture. "I bet your parents were so proud."

"My mom passed away just before Thanksgiving my first year of college, and my dad, well, he wasn't impressed with my career choice." Noah didn't like talking about his family, so he quickly changed the subject. "This guy standing on the end here is Lance Arvani."

Maddy leaned closer to get a better look. "He doesn't look familiar," she said. "Of course, no one looks familiar at this point, right?"

He felt bad for her. Not having a memory, good or bad, had to be difficult. "Speaking of which, did you look in the pictures folder to see if you have any of your family on here?"

"No, I didn't think of that. I was focused on Pietro."

Clicking on the photos folder revealed it was empty. He frowned. "That's weird. You're very close to your family. It seems odd you don't have pictures of them on here."

"Maybe it's a work computer."

He glanced over at her. "Yeah, probably. At least you'll see your brother later today. I'm sure seeing your twin will restore your memory."

"I hope so," she agreed. "Back to Arvani, what else can we find out about him?"

Noah took control of the keyboard, searching on Arvani's name. "His last known address is in a suburb north of Chicago."

"That doesn't help much," she groused.

He tried several other searches using different key phrases, but still nothing came up. He sat back in his seat. "I wonder if Arvani's working undercover."

"What makes you think that?"

He glanced at Maddy. "Consider the theory that Arvani was working as an undercover narcotics officer. Maybe he got greedy and turned dirty. Or maybe that's just his cover, a way to get close to working with Pietro."

She pursed her lips, considering the angle. "I thought undercover cops didn't use their real names? If he was known to be a cop, why would anyone from Pietro's organization trust him?"

"Good point," he conceded. "Going undercover usually involves a new name and cover story. But there's always the possibility that Arvani did something, or got caught with product owned by Pietro, so the organization is using that information to blackmail him."

She turned to face him, her knees pressing against his. "You want him to be a good guy, huh?"

"Not particularly," he argued. "We weren't friends or anything. I'm trying to understand why a cop's name would be linked to Pietro as a known associate."

"Would help if I could remember," Maddy said with a glum expression. "I really thought my memory would have returned by now."

"It will," he said reassuringly. He reached out to take her small hand in his. "In a few hours we'll meet up with Matt and I'm convinced he'll help you to remember."

She smiled and tilted her head. "Noah, do you mind if I ask you a personal question?"

Personal? His heart thudded against his rib cage with such force, he was surprised the cracked ribs didn't give way. His mouth was dry, but he managed to return her smile. "Of course not. What do you want to know?"

"Do you have a girlfriend?" The words came out in a breathless rush. "I'm only asking because you've been with me all night and I think she'd want to know you're okay."

For a moment, his mind flashed back to the last time

he saw Gina, how upset she'd been when he'd broken up with her.

How she'd gone out to party, using prescription drugs and alcohol, and had been found unresponsive and ultimately brain-dead.

"No." He pushed the word past his tight throat. "I don't have a girlfriend. I'm not good with relationships."

Her expression turned sympathetic. "Someone hurt you badly, huh?"

"No, you have it all wrong." He pulled away, leaping to his feet with such force his chair toppled over backward. "*I'm* the one who hurts *them*."

She looked surprised by that, and he could tell she wanted to ask more questions.

Not happening. He needed to go. To get away. "Excuse me," he said, making a beeline for the connecting door.

He dropped down on the edge of his bed, cradling his head in his hands. The memories of his sister's death, followed two and a half years later by Gina's passing, would never go away.

In truth he didn't want them to. If he'd been a better brother to Rose, a better boyfriend to Gina, maybe things would have turned out differently.

Once Maddy regained her memory, she'd remember how much she didn't like him. But even if her feelings had softened toward him, it didn't matter. Better for her to understand that no matter how much he cared about her, there could never be anything but friendship between them.

Maddy watched with dismay as Noah bolted to his adjoining room. She hated that her lack of memory had caused him pain.

No way did she believe Noah was the type to hurt women, especially not physically. Emotionally? Maybe, she didn't know him, or remember enough, to say for sure either way.

Yet his claim didn't make sense when he'd been nothing but kind to her since he'd come to see her in the ER. More than kind. Sweet. Compassionate. Supportive.

Protective.

No, she wasn't buying it. There had to be more to the story. Unfortunately, Noah had made it clear he wasn't going to clue her in.

Her back went ramrod straight as a horrible thought hit her. What if Noah was talking about the two of them? That he'd done something to ruin their relationship? After all, from the moment she first saw him, she'd been struck by how handsome he was.

As if he was the type of guy she normally was attracted to. Was it possible they were seeing each other?

No, surely if there had been something more than friendship between them, he would have said something? Her memory was nothing but pea soup anyway. Why not give her a high-level but condensed version of what had transpired between them?

None of it made any sense, so she told herself to focus on the case.

A case she couldn't remember.

Frustrated tears pricked her eyelids. She quickly blinked them back, refusing to wallow in self-pity. Her headache was better after her brief nap, but staring at the computer screen seemed to make it worse, so she quickly shut it down.

"I'm sorry."

Noah's quiet words had her spinning around in surprise. "For what?"

"Walking away like that. It's something my dad used to do when he got angry and I promised myself I wouldn't be like that." Noah stepped across the threshold of their connecting rooms. "Please accept my apology."

She rose to her feet. "I think I'm the one who should apologize for poking my nose into your personal life. But I want you to know, Noah, I'm here if you want to talk."

He dropped his gaze as if embarrassed. "Thanks, but we have bigger issues to worry about. If you're feeling up to it, I'd like to head out and pick up a couple of prepaid phones."

The thought of heading out into the cold held little appeal. Through the window she could see the sun was shining, but at the truck stop across the street people were bundled up against the cold, their breath steaming in front of their faces. She shivered just thinking about the cold. "Do you really think there's something within walking distance?"

"I was thinking of calling a taxi. I'd rather use a car service because they're much cheaper, but I can't do that without a phone and credit card. Still, it can't cost too much to get to the nearest big-box store. And if there's anything else you need, we can get everything in one fell swoop."

"Are you sure you have enough cash?" He'd purchased a toothbrush and hairbrush for her already, along with the warm fleece she was currently wearing. Offhand, she couldn't think of anything else she desperately needed. But she understood why he wanted a phone.

"Just enough, but I'll need more, soon."

"Sure, I'm glad to go."

"All right then. Be ready to leave in five."

She used the time to freshen up in the bathroom, before donning her coat. Maybe if there was enough cash left over, they could pick up a couple of hats, gloves and a nice warm scarf, too.

"Ready?" Noah stood waiting by the door. She noticed

he had his uniform back on, including the vest that had saved his life.

"What about the computer and the rest of our things? Isn't it better to take everything with us, just in case?"

He hesitated, then nodded. "You're right. In fact, it's probably better if we don't come back here at all."

Leaving the warmth of the motel room for good hadn't been her intention, but she couldn't deny that moving from one place to the next was smarter than staying put.

Stuffing their meager items into the computer case and the convenience store bag didn't take long. She carried the plastic bag, leaving Noah to sling the computer case over his shoulder.

Before they left the room, though, he crossed over and picked up the phone. He dialed a number, then spoke quickly.

"Milwaukee Police Officer Jackson Dellis was murdered at the Racine Marina." He paused, listening, then said, "No, I'm sorry but I can't give you my name. Trust me, send a squad to the marina."

He hung up the phone, capturing her gaze. "I had to call it in," he said defensively. "I waited till now, so that we'll be long gone before the cops trace the call."

"I'm not arguing with you, Noah."

"Thanks." He led the way outside without saying anything more.

Noah hailed a taxi and soon they were on the road, the motel growing smaller behind them. The driver seemed a bit intimidated by Noah's uniform, judging by the way he kept glancing at them in the rearview mirror, but he didn't say anything.

After sliding out of the back seat, she glanced at Noah. "Do you think he'll call the police?"

Noah smirked. "Why would he? I am the police."

His teasing tone made her smile. "I know that, and you know that, but he probably thinks you're pretending to be a cop. Otherwise, why would you need a taxi?"

"Because my squad car is in Lake Michigan," he said, tucking his hand beneath her elbow. "I'm not worried about the driver calling anyone. He has no reason to be suspicious and won't want to cause trouble. Come on, let's get inside."

Having Noah beside her was nice, and she noticed several people glanced at them curiously as they entered the store. Because he was in uniform? Or because he was so attractive?

Both, she decided.

The store was playing Christmas music and there were dozens of shoppers milling around. Noah headed for the electronics section first, choosing two disposable phones. "I'm not sure I need one," she said in a low voice. "Can't call people I don't remember."

"You'll remember soon," he said, tucking the packages into their cart. "Are you sure you don't want anything else?"

"Maybe gloves and a scarf, if we have enough cash left over."

"Not a problem. This way." He wheeled the cart down another aisle, taking her past the craft section.

A large glossy book on knitting caught her eye. She stopped, reaching out to touch the cover. It looked familiar.

The memory fragment was there, hovering just out of reach. She knew she'd seen this book before, but where? She pressed her fingertips to her temples, willing herself to remember.

"Maddy? Something wrong?"

The foggy image of this book sitting on a coffee table faded away, leaving behind a frustrated sense of urgency.

She had something important to do. Related to the trial? She didn't know.

"Maddy?" Noah lightly grasped her arm. "What's wrong? Is your memory returning?"

"Not really. For a moment I had an image of this book sitting on a coffee table, but that's it. Nothing helpful."

He slid his arm around her waist, giving her a hug. "I'm sorry, but let's take this as a good sign. Fragments of memories are better than nothing. This may be just the beginning."

She leaned her head against his shoulder for a moment, breathing in his reassuring woodsy scent. "Yeah, I hope so."

He surprised her by pressing a kiss to the top of her head. "Maybe we should wander around the store some more, see if anything else looks familiar."

She smiled and shook her head. "Doubtful. Let's find those gloves and scarves, okay?"

The items were fairly picked over, maybe because Christmas was only three weeks away. She didn't care if the items were mismatched as long as they were warm.

After paying for their items, she ripped the tags off the gloves, hat and scarf and put them on. Noah did the same, and the few items helped her feel warmer when they went back outside.

"How about we get a bite to eat over there?" Noah gestured to a family-style restaurant. "We have an hour or so before we need to head over to the bowling alley."

"Sounds good."

The place was busy, maybe because of the holiday season, but they only waited a few minutes before being seated in a booth near the window. She felt self-conscious carrying all their stuff, but then realized that it probably looked as if they'd been out Christmas shopping.

Their server was a young woman who smiled and introduced herself as Cindy. Maddy ordered coffee and Noah raised a brow questioningly, even though he asked for the same. The menu was basic fare, so she opted for a veggie burger while he requested beef.

"What?" she asked, when their server went to enter their order. "Don't I like coffee?"

He shrugged. "There's a coffeemaker in your condo, but I can't say for sure if you use it or Gretchen does."

Cindy returned, filling both of their mugs with coffee. Maddy didn't hesitate to add cream and sugar, before taking a sip. "Aah, that hits the spot."

"You ordered hot chocolate earlier," he said, cradling his own mug. "Did you remember liking coffee?"

"I wish. No, earlier hot chocolate sounded good, but this time, I wanted coffee." She shrugged. "I'm still tired, could use something to help wake me up a bit."

"Or maybe, subconsciously, your memory is starting to return."

She stared down at her cup for a moment. Was Noah right? Were little pieces of her previous life instinctively coming back to her? First the knitting book, avoiding meat and now adding cream and sugar to her coffee?

The small flicker of hope burned brighter. She knew that with God's love and support, anything was possible.

"More coffee?" Cindy asked. "Your food will be ready shortly."

Maddy nodded. Their server wasn't kidding. Five minutes later, she brought out two sandwich plates, one veggie, both with a mountain of french fries. Maddy placed her napkin in her lap, then reached for Noah's hand.

"Let's pray," she said.

His warm fingers wrapped around hers, and he bowed his head, waiting for her to start.

"Dear Lord, we thank You for this food we are about to eat. We also ask that You continue healing our wounds, Noah's bruises and my lost memory. Amen."

"Amen," Noah echoed. He raised his head and looked at her, continuing to hold her hand in his. "That was nice."

She smiled. "I'm glad."

The food was delicious, although there was no way in the world she could eat that many fries. When they finished, Noah paid Cindy, including a tip.

"Maybe we should have skipped breakfast. How much cash do you have left?" Maddy asked, winding her new scarf around her neck.

"Less than eighty bucks," Noah admitted with a wry grimace. "But I'm sure Matt will bring some with him."

Matt. The twin brother she couldn't remember.

This time, it took longer to grab a taxi but the bowling alley was only ten miles away. Maddy watched as Noah paid, feeling bad that she was unable to contribute.

"Let's head over to the coffee shop. We can see the entire parking lot from there."

She nodded in agreement, then put her hand on his arm, stopping him from walking away. "Noah?"

He met her gaze. "What? Is there something you need?"

"You're going to think I'm crazy, but I need a hug."

His mouth dropped open as if stunned speechless, but then he covered his reaction by wrapping his arms around her and pulling her close. "Hey, everything is going to be fine, you'll see."

She wanted desperately to believe that. But deep down, she was afraid that her twin would arrive and she wouldn't remember anything.

After several moments, Noah loosened his grip. "Okay now?"

She tipped her head back to look up at him. Being held

in his arms was so nice—she couldn't remember feeling like this before. His gaze held hers questioningly, but instead of telling him, she did what she'd wanted to do since she saw him in the emergency room. Lifting herself up on her toes, she pressed her mouth against his.

SEVEN

At first, Noah was taken aback by Maddy's unexpected kiss, but then his instincts took over and he crushed her close, deepening the embrace. She felt so right in his arms, tasting like a mixture of coffee, cinnamon, sunshine and juniper.

Like Christmas.

If he were honest with himself, he'd dreamed of kissing her, since way back when he and Matthew first became partners. But he didn't do relationships, even back then, and regardless he'd known she was off-limits.

Off-limits!

Reality kicked hard and he broke away, breathing heavily. "Uh, Maddy, we shouldn't be doing this," he managed.

"Why? You said yourself, you don't have a girlfriend."

"I don't." But then again, she might be seeing someone. The thought was sobering. She hadn't mentioned dating anyone during the trial prep, but she'd also been focused solely on the case. "And I explained why. I don't do relationships."

"Could have fooled me with that kiss," she responded tartly. "And don't bother handing me that line about how you're the one who hurts others." She angled her chin in that stubborn way she had. "Because I'm not buying it."

"Trust me, you won't be happy about this once your memory returns." He resisted the urge to pull her back into his arms, instead forcing himself to take a step back, putting more distance between them, at least physically.

Mentally was another story. There was no way he'd be able to get her out of his head; at least, not anytime soon.

"Noah," she started, but he cut her off.

"Let's get inside. Your brother should be here in less than twenty minutes."

Hopefully, he added silently. *Please, Lord, please send Matt to help.*

Maddy walked ahead of him into the café, her head held high. He reminded himself how terrible he was at relationships. How he was responsible for Gina's death. And how even if Maddy might be interested now, she surely wouldn't be once she remembered everything.

Yet her taste lingered on his mouth, taunting him with what he'd never have.

He'd been knocked off balance since the moment he'd recognized her in the ER. And if anything, they'd only grown closer as they fled from danger. He'd always admired her dedication to her career, but being with her like this had shown him another side of her. Her strength, even when she was exhausted. Her caring and compassion, when she'd realized his vest had stopped a bullet. Her sweetness when she'd kissed him.

And especially the way she'd prayed with him in the restaurant. He'd been humbled by her instinctive faith, remembering the way he'd often attended church services with the Callahan family.

After Matthew had been stabbed, his former partner's decision to attend K-9 training instead had eroded the closeness they'd once shared. Oh, sure, Matt had reached out a few times, asking Noah to join his family at church followed by his mother's famous brunch, but the thought of sitting around the dining room table with them, knowing they had every right to blame him for Matt's injury, had kept him far, far away.

Until now. Being sent to the ER to take Maddy's statement about the assault must have been God's way of protecting her. Noah firmly believed Matt would show at the bowling alley. And if he couldn't, Noah was certain he'd send one of the other Callahans in his place.

Any one of Maddy's brothers would likely restore her memory. Which would be a good thing, since he wanted—no, needed to know she'd be safe at last.

The Callahans always protected their own.

"Are you interested in more coffee?" she asked, breaking into his thoughts. "I think we should buy something if we're going to sit here."

He nodded. "What would you like?"

"Chamomile tea," she responded. "I think I've had enough caffeine for the day."

The request for tea surprised him. Then again, he truly didn't know what Maddy usually ate or drank. She assumed they were closer than they were, and he needed to tell her the truth, regardless of the fact that doing so would ruin the camaraderie they shared.

Feeling grim, he placed their order and paid, grimacing at his dwindling cash reserves. One of the Callahans better show, or they'd be in trouble. He didn't have enough cash to pay for another motel room. Especially if he needed to pay for a taxi ride to get there.

Carrying his coffee in one hand and her chamomile tea in the other, he joined her at a two-top table near the window overlooking the parking lot.

"Tell me about her," Maddy said, holding on to her tea with both hands.

"Who?"

"The girl who broke your heart."

His sister's face flashed into his brain. Losing Rose to a heroin overdose had been heartbreaking, but he knew that wasn't what Maddy meant. She was talking about Gina. He stalled, taking a sip of coffee, only to burn his tongue with the scalding hot brew. "I told you, it was the other way around. I was the one to break things off."

And Gina had died as a result of his rejection.

"Noah, the pain in your eyes tells a different story," she said gently. "Maybe she didn't break your heart, but she still hurt you."

"No, actually, she hurt herself. I broke up with her on a Friday night and she was found dead the next morning."

"No," Maddy said with a gasp and he grimaced, realizing he should have tried to soften the blow. His stomach knotted, but he continued sitting there, figuring it was better she knew the truth. "Suicide?"

"Accidental prescription-drug overdose mixed with alcohol or suicide. What's the difference? Dead is dead. Either way it was my fault."

Maddy rested her hand on his upper arm, her expression earnest. "Noah, you can't seriously believe you're responsible for her actions."

He couldn't sit there a moment longer. "Excuse me," he said, sliding off his chair. Her hand fell to her side and ridiculously enough, he immediately missed her touch. "I'm going to use the outlet over there to charge up and activate one of the phones."

Thankfully, she didn't try to stop him. At least now, Maddy knew the truth. There would be no more hugging or kissing, regardless of how much he yearned for that closeness.

Once Matt arrived, he could extricate himself from his role of her bodyguard and focus his efforts on finding out who had killed his partner and was trying to hurt Maddy.

Maddy watched Noah deal with their new phones, reeling from the news of his girlfriend's death. He was right, accidental overdose or suicide, the end result had been the same.

But why did he feel responsible? Couples broke up all the time for a variety of reasons. Growing apart and wanting different things from life, or maybe infidelity.

She sipped her tea, enjoying the soothing effect it had on her nerves. Noah didn't seem like the type of guy to cheat on his girlfriend; then again, maybe he'd broken things off because he'd found someone else. That was the sort of thing that could send a woman over the edge of despair. Although taking drugs and alcohol had been a conscious decision on her part, not Noah's.

Their mutual response to their kiss had convinced Maddy there was definitely something between them. Attraction at the very least.

There was no denying she'd hoped that kissing Noah would cause a spontaneous return of her memory, but it hadn't. Because they'd never kissed before? Possibly.

She stared out the window, watching cars coming and going. Would she instinctively recognize her brother when he arrived? How embarrassing if she didn't.

Propping her elbows on the table, she pressed her fingertips against her temples. Her headache had never truly gone away, but at times like this, when she tried to concentrate on remembering the past, the intensity of her pain increased exponentially.

She closed her eyes for a moment and silently asked for God's blessing.

"Are you okay?" Noah asked, his voice near her ear. He wrapped his arm around her shoulders as if afraid she'd fall off her stool. "What can I do?"

She looked up at him with a soft smile. "I'm fine."

"You don't look fine," he said bluntly, his brown eyes mirroring concern. She liked having his arm around her and allowed herself a moment to lean against him, soaking up his strength. "I still have that bottle of ibuprofen. You should take some."

"I can do that," she agreed. He moved away from her, so she straightened her shoulders, determined not to be weak. Watching as he dug through their bag of belongings, she knew this was exactly why she didn't believe he'd intentionally set out to hurt anyone. He'd been upset about her probing into his past, but the moment he thought she needed help, he'd come rushing over to offer assistance, putting her needs before his.

"Here." He opened the bottle and shook a couple pills into her palm. "This should help."

"I hope so." She tossed them back and took a sip of her tea. "Of course it might also help if I stopped trying so hard to remember."

His smile was lopsided. "Have faith, Maddy. Your memory will return when your brain is ready."

"My brother won't appreciate me not remembering him," she pointed out.

"Your brothers love you, Maddy. You're very close to them. I promise, they're not going to hold a bit of amnesia against you."

"So tell me, Noah, how is it that you know so much about me and my family?" She held his gaze, hoping he'd fill the gaps. "You and I haven't dated, have we?"

His eyes widened comically. "No! Of course not."

She couldn't help but wonder why. Especially given this underlying attraction that relentlessly simmered between them. "But you helped me and my roommate move into our condo," she pressed. "So we must be friends."

He hesitated, then nodded. "Yes, we're friends. In fact, your brother Matt used to be my partner."

Hearing that surprised her. "Used to be? What happened?"

He paused for so long she thought he wasn't going to answer. Then he finally let out a heavy sigh, and met her gaze. "A little over a year ago now, Matt was injured on the job." His tone was full of resignation, as if this story was somehow painful to tell. "He was stabbed during a drug bust. When he recovered, he decided to pursue his dream of K-9 training."

She sensed there was more he wasn't telling her, but decided not to push. "What kind of dog does he have?"

A smile tugged at the corner of his mouth. "A German shepherd named Duchess. He's done an incredible job with her. The two of them are amazing to watch."

"Maybe he'll bring Duchess along today," she said, glancing at her watch. Ten minutes until four o'clock. "I'd love to meet her." Then she flushed. "Well, I guess I've already met her, huh?"

"Yes," he said gently. "But you need to stop beating yourself up about your memory loss. This isn't your fault."

"I will if you will," she countered.

He frowned. "If I will what?"

"Stop beating yourself up for the choices your girlfriend made the night she died."

Instantly his face turned to stone. "You don't seem to understand that I am responsible. My actions caused her reaction. Your amnesia is the result of an assault. Two completely different scenarios."

She didn't agree, but apparently Noah wasn't interested in further discussion on the topic. So she let it go, turning her attention to the parking lot.

Dusk was beginning to fall, the days growing shorter and shorter as the winter solstice approached. A black sedan pulled in and she straightened in her seat when she noticed a dog in the back of the vehicle.

"Is that him?" she asked, pointing toward the car.

Noah frowned. "I don't think so."

"Maybe you should call him."

Noah picked up the phone he'd just activated and punched in a series of numbers. He placed the call on speaker, and they both listened as it rang. She was glad he knew her brother's number by heart, since she, of course, had no idea.

"Yeah?" A male voice answered.

"Matt? It's Noah Sinclair."

"Where's Maddy? Are you both okay?" Concern edged Matt's tone.

"Don't worry, we're fine. Are you coming to meet us? What are you driving these days?"

"Should be there in less than five. I'm driving a black SUV." There was a pause, then Matt asked, "Maddy's with you, right?"

"I'm here," she said, speaking up for the first time. The sound of her brother's voice didn't bring on a tumble of memories, the way she'd hoped. "Noah has been doing a great job of protecting me."

"Good. Glad you're getting along," Matt said. "I'll see you both soon, okay?"

"Okay." She smiled gratefully at Noah, watching as he disconnected the call. "He sounds nice."

"Nice?" Noah chuckled. "I'd like to hear you say that to Matt's face. You'll always stick up for each other, but at the same time, you can squabble worse than a couple of five-year-olds."

Noah's description filled her with yearning. She wished so much that she could remember.

Her tea had gone cold, but she finished it off anyway. Noah had barely touched his coffee. The way he watched the parking lot, sweeping his gaze over the area, made her nervous.

Surely he didn't think they'd be ambushed here? No, it was more likely that he was just being a cop.

The minutes ticked by with excruciating slowness, but then a large black K-9 SUV pulled into the parking lot, the twin headlights bright amid the dusky shadows.

She couldn't get a good look at the man behind the wheel. After wrapping her scarf around her neck and pulling on her gloves, she slid off her seat. Noah had already grabbed their stuff, so she headed for the door. Noah moved lightning-fast, grasping her arm, halting her progress.

"Hold on a minute, Maddy." He pushed her behind him. "I'm going first, just in case."

Remembering how Jackson had been gunned down, she swallowed hard and nodded. She didn't want Noah in harm's way, either, but he was wearing the vest that had saved his life once before. She grasped the back of his utility belt, determined to follow close on his heels.

Outside, she barely noticed the cold air, her gaze centered on the black SUV she could see parked in a spot that was facing the bowling alley. The driver-side door opened and a tall, lithe man with hair so dark it looked black climbed out. Her brother turned and the moment she saw his face, the missing puzzle pieces clicked into place.

Matt! She let go of Noah and rushed around him in a hurry to reach her brother. "I remember you, Matt! I remember everything!"

"Get down!" Noah shouted just before the boom of a gun echoed through the parking lot.

Her brother reacted instinctively, covering Maddy and shoving her down to the ground. Noah ran over, crouching beside them.

"Where did the shot come from?" Matt asked, his voice tense.

"The three o'clock position. Get around to the front of the vehicle," Noah rasped. "Hurry, I'll cover."

"No, wait!" Maddy shouted, but it was too late. Noah turned to fire in the direction where the gunshot came from at the same time Matt yanked her around the open door, to the relative shelter of the front of the SUV.

Thankfully, Noah joined them a few seconds later. She pushed past Matt to check Noah for signs of injury.

"We need to call for backup," her brother said in a low voice.

"Not yet. There must be some sort of bug on your phone," Noah pointed out. "I'm positive we weren't followed and I called you with a brand-new disposable phone."

Matt's expression turned grim, and Maddy glanced between the two men. Oddly enough, there was no more gunfire, and she once again felt the sense of urgency.

"We need to get out of here," she whispered.

Matt and Noah exchanged a long look, ignoring her.

"Give me your keys," Noah said. "I'll get behind the wheel first. See if I can draw his fire."

"I'll do it," Matt said. "Duchess is in the back. She doesn't know you."

"I'm wearing a vest," Noah pointed out.

"I'll be fine." Matt didn't wait for Noah's response, but quickly rolled beneath the door, coming up and diving into the front seat. The move was quick and unexpected and no gunfire erupted as a result.

Noah grasped Maddy's hand. "Matt is going to slowly back up and turn around so that the truck is between us and the gunman," he said in a low voice. "Once he's turned, we'll get in the back of the cab, okay?"

"Got it," she agreed.

Matt already had the SUV rolling backward, angling to the side so that the front of the truck was pointing toward the exit. She and Noah moved as one, keeping pace with the vehicle while staying crouched down.

"Now," Noah said when the SUV was perpendicular to the parking spot.

She yanked open the back door and crawled inside. Noah tossed their stuff in, then clambered in behind her. He'd barely shut the door when Matt hit the accelerator.

Still no gunfire. Had Noah's return fire scared them off? The seconds stretched into a full minute before Matt said, "We're all clear."

"Thank You, Lord," Maddy whispered, relaxing back into the seat, grateful to God for keeping them safe. Then her eyes flew open. "Matt! We need to check on Mom and Nan."

Her twin, his face now as familiar as her own, caught her gaze in the rearview mirror. "Why?"

She swallowed hard. "I was attacked outside the courthouse. The man who grabbed me told me to drop the case or everyone I cared about would die, including the two old ladies living on the hill." The words came out in a rush. "Don't you see? Mom and Nan live in the old colonial house on the top of Brookmont Ridge. They're both in danger."

"They were fine when I spoke to them yesterday," Matt said. "But I can call to check on them now."

"No, don't use your phone," Noah warned. "Not until we figure out how in the world Pietro's men knew our meeting place."

Maddy pressed her hand against her stomach, feeling sick. She needed, desperately, to know her mother and grandmother were safe.

If they were harmed in any way, she'd never forgive herself. *Never.*

EIGHT

Noah was thankful they'd gotten away from the parking lot, but his instincts were still screaming at him about the level of danger. He twisted in his seat to keep an eye out for anyone who might be following, only to come face to face with Matt's K-9 partner, Duchess.

"Hey, Duchess. Remember me?" He put his hand near the crate bars for the dog to sniff. Looking past the animal, he could see several pairs of headlights behind them.

Could one of them be the shooter?

The dog sniffed his hand, then wagged her tail. He turned his attention back to the issue at hand. "Matt, there's a chance the shooter has your license plate number."

"I know." Matt didn't sound at all happy about the possibility. "It's not as if a K-9 SUV is easy to disguise, either."

"Noah, I need to use your new phone to call my mom," Maddy said. "I can't bear the thought that Pietro's goons have their house staked out."

Noah hesitated, not because he wanted to deny Maddy's request—he certainly understood her need to know her mother and grandmother were safe—but because he'd used his phone to call Matt. Disposable cell phones weren't easy to trace, but he knew it was possible. Especially if Pietro had someone working for him within law enforcement.

"Noah, please!" Maddy's voice rose with agitation.

"Hold on, Maddy," Matt said. "Don't call Mom directly. It's better if we call Miles and send him over there to check on them."

"Why is that any different?" Maddy asked, clearly frustrated.

"Because Miles is a homicide detective," Noah reminded her. "We can call Dispatch and ask to have the call sent directly to him. If the call is traced, they'll know only that we called the police, not specifically who within the department."

"Fine. Call Dispatch, then. But hurry," Maddy said.

Noah made the call, requesting to be connected to Miles Callahan's number. Unfortunately, the detective didn't pick up. He left a message telling Miles to go directly to his mother's house to ensure their safety. But he knew Maddy wouldn't be satisfied with that.

"Send a squad over there," she demanded. "I want a wellness check."

"Okay." Noah made the second call, wondering if the terseness of Maddy's tone was related to her memory return. She'd been antagonistic toward him at the hospital after Matt's injury, standing at her twin's bedside as if she was his personal bodyguard. Two days earlier, she'd profusely thanked him for helping her and Gretchen move into their new condo, so he knew her icy attitude had been because she blamed him for Matt's injury.

"Officer Matt Callahan is requesting a wellness check on his mother and grandmother," he told the dispatcher. "Please send a squad to the premises ASAP."

"Will do, officer," the dispatcher responded.

Noah didn't bother to correct her assumption that he was actually Matt. Right now the important thing was to make sure that Matt and Maddy's mother and grandmother were safe. Besides, he wasn't so sure he wanted the dispatcher to know who he was. He'd left the anonymous tip about Jackson's murder, but did they also know about his squad car being submerged in Lake Michigan? He had to believe they would put the two issues together and realize he was either in trouble or had gone rogue, killing his own partner.

After all, it wasn't a huge leap. His reputation related to keeping a partner safe was already ruined. Jackson's death would be the final nail in that coffin.

His career was likely so far down in the gutter there was no hope of recovery. His chest tightened painfully and he struggled to draw a deep breath.

What would he do without his career? He had no idea.

"Thank you, Noah," Maddy said, derailing his thoughts by resting her hand on his arm. "I appreciate your sending the squad to check on Mom and Nan."

"Ah, sure." He was nonplussed by the note of sincerity in her tone. "I completely understand. I want them to be safe, too."

She squeezed his arm. "I know you do."

He stared at her pale fingers, wondering why she was being so nice to him. Maybe for Matt's benefit? That was the only thing that made sense, now that her memory had returned.

"Where to?" Matt asked, interrupting them. "I'm doing my best to make sure I'm not being followed, but it would be nice to have a destination in mind."

"I'm not sure," Noah admitted. Maddy let go of his arm and he had to curb his desire to reach out to clasp her hand in his. "A motel would be best. It's likely that the police are searching for me, so I don't think it's smart to head back to my place. Too much has happened, I'm worried they'll arrest me first and ask questions later."

"Why would they arrest you?" Matt's questioning gaze met his. "What's really going on here?"

"My partner, Jackson Dellis, was murdered earlier this morning. He was shot because I called him and asked him to pick us up at the Racine Marina."

Matt whistled between his teeth. "That's not good. Although it's strange, I didn't hear anything in the news about a murder victim being found in that area. Usually the reporters are all over that kind of thing."

In Noah's opinion, the media were bloodsucking leeches, but hey, all in the name of freedom of speech, right? He'd never forget how relentlessly awful they were the day after his sister died. "Maybe you missed it. Trust me, it's probably being broadcast as we speak. In fact, we were fortunate to get away from the marina in one piece."

"Noah took a bullet in the back," Maddy chimed in, once again coming to his defense. "Thankfully, he was wearing his vest."

Matt's expression darkened for a moment, then he gave a terse nod. "Thanks for saving Maddy's life, Noah. I owe you for that."

He shifted in his seat, uncomfortable with Matt's gratitude. "It's nothing. But I'm sorry to tell you I'm out of cash. I hope you'll lend me some."

"There's no lending involved," Maddy interjected. "You've already paid for our meals, clothing, phones and the rooms at the last motel. I need to pay my fair share."

"I have plenty of cash," Matt said. "No need to worry about who owes whom. The important thing is to keep Maddy safe while we figure out who Pietro hired to kill her."

"Yes, I know he's the one behind this, but don't forget, I have a trial to prepare for," Maddy reminded him, a stubborn edge to her voice. "So really, the most important thing is to keep Mom and Nan safe. I need to get to my office."

"I don't think that's a good idea," Noah said, striving for patience. "Pietro already made one attempt on you at the courthouse. Why would you give him access to a second attempt? What if he succeeds next time?"

Maddy drew away from him as if he'd hurt her. "Why on earth would I cave in to his pathetic attempts to derail the trial? Prosecuting this case has only gotten more important in the past twenty-four hours. I won't let him chase me away from doing my job."

Noah inwardly groaned at the way she folded her arms across her chest and thrust out her chin. Stubborn Maddy was back.

At least Memory Loss Maddy had agreed to follow his lead in keeping her safe. Now, protecting her from harm would only be more difficult.

If not downright impossible.

Maddy turned away from Noah, staring sightlessly out the passenger-side window. She'd expected Matt to give her a hard time about moving forward with the trial, but not Noah.

She'd thought they'd connected on a deeper, more personal level over the past several hours.

Since their heated kiss.

Then again, Noah had been the one to pull away from their embrace. Her cheeks went pink with embarrassment at the memory. Kissing him in the first place had been out of character for her. Now that her memory had returned, she knew just how much she'd avoided men since the night four months ago she'd been groped by one of her colleagues, who'd thought he was the catch of the century.

Yeah, so *not*.

She hadn't told anyone, especially not her brothers, about that night, about how scared she'd been deep down in her heart that Blake Ratcliff would force her against her will. He'd had her pinned against the desk in his office, blocking the doorway, holding her against him. Fortunately, a security guard had come on his rounds outside Blake's office. He'd knocked sharply on the door, asking if everything was all right. Blake had let her go, and she'd used the opportunity to escape unscathed.

Mostly unscathed. For weeks afterward, she'd had trouble putting the event behind her, doing her best to focus instead on her career.

Alexander Pietro's case had been a good distraction, but she'd continued looking over her shoulder, afraid she'd find herself targeted once again by Ratcliff.

"I have to agree with Noah," Matt said from the front seat. "You can't just stroll into your office, Maddy."

She tossed her head, glaring at him. "Oh, really? As if you or any of our other brothers would ever let something like this stop you from doing your job. Just because you happen to be in some area of law enforcement doesn't make you bulletproof. Miles and Marc were shot last year while protecting their witnesses. And you were stabbed just a few months before Marc's injury."

Noah flinched beside her, and for a moment she regretted adding that last part. Not that it wasn't true, because it was. And yeah, she'd blamed Noah for Matt's injury for weeks afterward. Until Matt confronted her, asking why she couldn't forgive him the way God taught them to.

So she'd done her best to do just that.

"Matt's wound was my fault, not his," Noah said. "And that's not the point. Neither one of us goes into dangerous situations without being prepared. Matt's right, you can't just stroll into work as if none of this happened."

They were ganging up on her, two against one. But they'd forgotten that she'd grown up with five older brothers and knew how to hold her own. "Then we'll find a way to prepare," she said. "I'm sure one of you can get me a vest, and between the two of you, provide round-the-clock protection. We need to find a way to make this work. If Pietro walks, all of this will have been for nothing. Including Jackson's murder."

Silence filled the vehicle, broken only by Duchess's movements and breathing. It seemed like hours, but was likely only a few minutes, before Noah spoke up.

"She's right, Matt. We can't let Pietro get away with this. In fact, there's no guarantee that he wouldn't continue to come after Maddy or the rest of your family, even if she did drop the case."

Her twin let out a heavy sigh. "Yeah, okay. But first we find a motel."

"And a new ride," Noah added. "I'm sorry, but I don't think we can safely use this one."

"I know." Matt took another turn and Maddy was surprised to see they were in front of a low-budget motel on the opposite side of town from where her mother and grandmother lived. Was that a good thing? She wasn't sure. She'd rather be close by, in case something happened. "I'll drop you off and return later with another vehicle."

"Thanks, Matt," Noah said. "Don't forget we need cash, too."

"I got it." He pushed out of the car and dug in his pocket. Noah slid out to join him, offering a hand to Maddy. She took it, allowing him to help her, struck again by his manners. Had Noah always been this courteous? To be fair, she'd always thought he was a nice-looking guy, but she hadn't been interested in getting involved with her brother's partner. And then, after the stabbing, she'd distanced herself from Noah even further.

Then Blake had put her off men, completely. Or so she'd thought.

Looking back over the time they'd spent together since Noah had come to her rescue at the hospital, she realized she'd never really known him on a personal level. The man who carried the guilt over his girlfriend's death like a yoke across his shoulders.

She gave herself a mental shake as she followed Matt inside the motel lobby. Noah had been nothing but kind and protective of her, but that didn't mean anything had changed between them. He still didn't want to become involved and frankly, she wasn't interested in a long-term relationship right now, either. The incident with Blake Ratcliff still bothered her, and her priority had to be on winning the case against Alexander Pietro, sending him to prison for a long, long time.

"They have adjoining rooms available," Noah said in a low voice. "So I told Matt to take them."

She nodded, thinking that it would be good to have her own space. Strange how being close to Noah hadn't bothered her when she'd had amnesia, but now she was a little relieved to have some separation between them. Not that Noah had ever acted the way Ratcliff had.

Still, remembering the way Blake had accused her of sending out vibes that she was interested in him made her wonder if maybe she had.

After all, she'd initiated the kiss with Noah, hadn't she?

When they were finished in the lobby, they headed back outside. "Here you go," Matt said, passing respective room keys to them. He also handed Noah a wad of cash. "It's ten minutes past five o'clock now. I plan to return no later than eight."

"Where are you going to get a spare ride?" Noah asked.

"Not sure," Matt admitted.

"Your friend Garrett is back from his deployment, isn't he?" Maddy asked. "So using his truck is probably out of the question."

"Garrett's a great guy. He may be willing to help out. If not, we have other friends. I'll find a way."

"I know you will," she agreed.

Matt stepped in and wrapped her in a bear hug. She clung to him for a moment, tears pricking her eyes. How could she have forgotten her twin? Her family? Her mother and grandmother?

"Stay safe," Matt whispered in her ear. "And be nice to Noah."

"I will." She hung on for another long moment, then released him. "See you later."

"Back at you." Matt slapped Noah on the shoulder. "Take care of my baby sis."

"Of course. Come on, Maddy, let's get inside." Noah gestured for Maddy to precede him toward their rooms, but she waited until Matt slid into the SUV and started up the engine, watching as he drove away.

Their rooms were nothing special; they were clean but smelled musty enough to make her wrinkle her nose. Still, it was warm and they were safe, so she wasn't about to complain. As she turned up the heater, there was a knock on the connecting door between their rooms.

She crossed over to unlock it. Noah stood there, holding out the plastic bag containing their personal items. "I took out my sweatshirt and toothbrush. The rest is yours."

"Thanks." She took the bag, then gestured toward the computer case. "What are you working on?"

"Nothing yet, but now that you have your memory back,

we should review your notes again. We still have Lance Arvani as a key suspect."

She winced. Under normal circumstances, Noah shouldn't know anything about Arvani. Although clearly there wasn't anything normal about being rammed into a lake or being shot at, not just once but three times. She needed to figure out a way to salvage the case, and how Noah had gotten dragged into the recent events, as well. "Give me a few minutes, okay?"

"Sure." Noah stepped back and closed his door halfway.

Maddy carried her personal items into the bathroom, using the time to freshen up. There were dark circles beneath her eyes; the restorative effect of the measly five hours of sleep she'd managed to grab was fading fast. The only good thing was that her headache wasn't nearly as bad as it had been, the level of pain such that it was easily ignored.

Ten minutes later, she entered Noah's room to find him searching the internet on the computer. "Find anything?" she asked, dropping into the seat beside him.

"No, and I don't like it."

She raised an eyebrow. "Okay, what exactly are you looking for? Something on Arvani?"

"No, on Jackson's murder." Noah cleared his current search and tried again, typing in the words *Racine Marina*.

She leaned in close, trying not to let Noah's masculine scent distract her as she watched various results fill the screen.

"I don't understand," Noah muttered. "The news of Jackson's death should be all over the place by now. A dead off-duty cop lying beside a car in a pool of blood wouldn't be overlooked."

She agreed. "Do you think it's possible that the police found him first and kept the whole thing under wraps?"

Noah shrugged, trying different key phrases in the search engine. "I left an anonymous call about it, so I guess it's possible, but I don't see why they would. After all, they probably already know about my squad car being in Lake Michigan, too. Surely they linked the two incidents."

"Maybe someone else moved the body?" Maddy said.

"And cleaned up all the blood? Not likely."

"Try searching on the squad car falling into Lake Michigan?" she suggested.

He did as she asked, and immediately several hits came up. Noah clicked on the top story with the headline Abandoned Police Vehicle Submerged in Lake Michigan.

Silently they both scanned the article. The reporter described the vehicle as being mostly submerged in the water before it was found and that foul play against the officer assigned to the vehicle was suspected. Strangely, the article didn't mention Noah Sinclair by name.

"It doesn't make sense," Noah said again. "They obviously have the story here on my squad car being found in the lake, but nothing related to my murdered partner? That's the bigger news story here. Not an empty police car. A man's death should be taking priority."

"Here, let me try." Maddy turned the laptop computer so that it was facing her directly. She tried several different search engines, along with different phrases, but without a single result.

It was as if Jackson's murder hadn't happened.

How was that possible?

She twisted toward Noah. "What if the shooter came down the hill and stuffed Jackson back in his car?" she asked. "A parked car might not raise anyone's suspicions. What if he's still out there?"

Noah's mouth thinned. "Anything is possible, although I still think someone would have gone searching for him by now. And if they'd found his home empty but his car gone from the garage, they would have put out an APB."

A chill rippled down her spine. "They would have done that for you, too, then, right?"

He nodded slowly. "Yeah, especially since they clearly found my car. Two missing cops, who were partners, had to have raised an alarm."

Her stomach twisted painfully. Jackson's body should have been found, in or out of his abandoned car. Even a bloodstain on the ground would normally have alerted someone.

Which meant Noah was right. The police had to be withholding the information from the media. And the likely reason to do that was because Noah himself had to be their prime suspect in the shooting death of his partner.

NINE

Noah could see by the resigned expression in Maddy's blue eyes that she understood the gravity of his situation. He grieved for the loss of his partner, the murder of a good cop, but that wasn't the only problem.

The more he thought about it, the more he realized this latest turn of events could not only harm his career, but the integrity of Maddy's case against Pietro.

He'd been involved in the bust and subsequent arrest of the narcotic crime boss. If he was being framed and was charged with murdering his partner, his credibility would go swirling down the drain. Why would a jury believe him?

Why would anyone?

A flash of hopelessness swept over him, and for a moment he wanted to rail at God about the unfairness of it all, but on the heels of that thought came a wave of shame.

No, this wasn't God's fault. Or Maddy's. Or his. Pietro was the one facing life in prison for murder and running a massive drug ring. Pietro was the one who hired someone to go after Maddy outside the courthouse. Pietro and his men were the ones behind the murder of Noah's partner and the multiple attempts to take him and Maddy out of the picture, permanently.

He and Maddy needed to figure out who was working for the imprisoned narcotic trafficker and soon. Before things spiraled even further out of control.

If Pietro went after Maddy's family, he was certain she'd hand the case off to another ADA. And really, Noah wouldn't blame her.

As far as the Callahans were concerned, family always came first.

"I think Arvani is the key," Maddy said, drawing his attention back to the immediate issue at hand. "I'm sure he's involved in this somehow."

Working the case in a constructive manner was better than wishing things were different. "Tell me how you know Arvani is a known associate of Pietro's in the first place? What links them together?"

Maddy sat for a moment, her brow furrowed as she picked through her memory. "I need my notes," she said, taking control of the computer keyboard. "I can't remember exactly why I linked them together. I don't believe I was aware of Arvani's background as a cop, and that doesn't make sense. Surely I would have checked him out?"

Noah knew Maddy was extremely thorough, so he remained silent, giving her the time she needed to review her notes. He watched her rather than the screen, thinking once again about how beautiful she was. Not just her physical features, but deep down, where it counted. He remembered the way she'd supported him when he'd explained how Gina had overdosed, by accident or on purpose after he'd broken up with her.

I will if you will.

He'd told her to stop beating herself up over something that wasn't her fault. And she'd told him, "I will if you will." But her memory loss wasn't exactly the same thing as him causing Gina's death. Was it?

No, of course not. Pietro sent someone after Maddy for the sole purpose of scaring her off the case, intentionally causing her harm.

He'd grown weary of Gina's constant neediness, the way she continued to call him incessantly if he didn't return her call right away. The way she always made a big deal out of nothing, imagining that other women were flirting with him, when they really weren't. Or accusing him of cheating on her. It seemed Gina wasn't happy without some sort of drama in her life.

Yet he should have been nicer about the whole thing, letting her down gently. Instead, he'd chosen to interrupt her in the middle of some tirade against a fellow student, abruptly telling her their relationship was over and that he didn't want to see her anymore.

Remembering how Gina had stumbled backward, as if he'd physically hit her, made him wince. She'd covered her mouth with her hand, tears welling in her eyes, before she'd turned and rushed out of his apartment.

And he'd done nothing to stop her.

He'd thought it was best to leave her alone. Wait until she calmed down before trying to talk to her, but that plan had backfired when she'd been found dead the next morning.

"Here," Maddy said, interrupting his internal rehashing of the past. "There was a phone call made from Pietro himself to Arvani's personal cell number. That was the only link I had between them."

That intrigued him. "When, exactly?"

"About a month before the bust. At the time, though, Arvani claimed his phone had been stolen. An allegation that had seemed possible considering he'd purchased a new phone the very next day, with a different number. Not to mention the fact that Arvani was in Chicago at the time but Pietro was here in Milwaukee."

Interesting, since Noah had suspected all along that Pietro was moving his criminal activities from Chicago to Milwaukee. "I'm not sure I believe that. Most phones are password protected," Noah said. "Seems improbable at best that some guy who just happens to be working with Pietro stole Arvani's phone and managed to break the code to use it."

"I agree," Maddy said. "Which is why I listed Arvani as a likely associate. I suspect there was some crisis that came up, causing Arvani to call Pietro directly, then he quickly ditched his phone and reported it stolen."

He liked the way her mind worked. "But you don't have Arvani being employed by the Chicago PD in your file?"

She grimaced and shook her head. "I was focusing on the trial prep. I gave the information I had to the detective working the case but didn't dig into it myself. There wasn't time. Pietro's lawyer was pushing for a quick trial after the judge denied bail."

Noah blew out a breath. "Okay, if we're right about Arvani working with Pietro, then what is our next step? There is a slight problem of jurisdiction, since we can't very well investigate a Chicago cop."

"We could get the FBI involved," Maddy said, her expression thoughtful. "My brother Marc is an agent in the Milwaukee branch of the bureau, and they don't have to worry about jurisdiction."

"We could, but we don't exactly have much evidence, either. A stolen phone and one call isn't much of a connection. But we could check on property owned by Arvani. Maybe he has something here in Wisconsin?"

"Good idea." Maddy went to work, her slender fingers

flying over the keys. He couldn't deny he liked sitting next to her like this, working a case together.

Whoa, get a grip, he told himself harshly. Liking Maddy as a friend, someone he cared about, was one thing; imagining some sort of future together was pure crazy talk.

"Noah! You were right!" Maddy turned and grabbed his arm. "Look, Lance Arvani owns a cabin on Willow Lake, just an hour outside of Milwaukee."

He stared at the information on the screen. "We need to check it out, see if we can find evidence that he's been spending time there."

"So what if he was?" Maddy countered logically. "That doesn't mean anything. What we really need is proof that he's working with Pietro."

"We can't legally enter the cabin without a search warrant," he pointed out.

"No, but it's worth driving by and checking the place out. If he's spending time there, I may be able to convince Judge Dugan to issue a search warrant."

"The trial is only five days away. Defense attorneys hate when new evidence is introduced so late in the proceedings."

"Yes, but that's their problem. We have a right to introduce new evidence as we find it." Maddy glanced at the clock on the bedside table. "We should be hearing from Matt shortly."

Noah glanced back at the address of Arvani's lake cabin, unable to suppress a surge of anticipation. The place might just give them the break they needed to get the local police or even the Feds involved.

It was possible, remotely possible, that proving Arvani's involvement in Pietro's drug dealing would not just solidify Maddy's case.

But salvage his career.

* * *

Maddy hated the thought of Noah being a suspect in his partner's murder. Hopefully, a trip out to Arvani's cabin would give them something, anything, to go on.

She scribbled Arvani's address on a scrap piece of paper, then clicked off the site. Where was her brother? He'd assured them he'd be back before eight o'clock, and it was quarter till by now.

"Don't worry, he'll be here soon," Noah said, as if he'd read her mind. "Matt won't leave you here without the ability to escape."

She forced a smile. "I know he wouldn't do that intentionally, but if he was followed or if something happened to my mom…" She couldn't finish.

Dear Lord, please keep Mom and Nan safe in Your care! Please!

"Hey, it's okay." Noah put his arm around her shoulders, giving her a brief hug. "Matt's a good cop. He can hold his own. And he has Duchess with him."

"True." She sighed and leaned against Noah, appreciating his support. "I just don't like feeling helpless."

"None of us do." His breath brushed against the hair near her temple.

She closed her eyes, savoring his embrace. It was odd how comfortable she felt with Noah. After Ratcliff's sneak attack, she had no interest in men. She had barely tolerated being alone in a room with them. Not easy when she'd been stuck preparing witnesses for trial for hours on end.

Back then, she'd been wary of Noah, too. But that fear of being close to a man hadn't been there during the time she'd been alone with him, first at the hospital, then in the squad, or at her condo. Wrapped in his arms on the boat, not once had she felt hemmed in, anxious to escape.

What did it all mean? That she'd subconsciously recognized Noah as someone she could trust? Even though she hadn't felt that way during their trial prep sessions?

She couldn't figure it out, unless this was the first step in the process of healing. Of forgiving Blake Ratcliff for what he'd done. Something she'd been praying about on a regular basis since that fateful night four months ago.

The memory was so fresh in her mind, it seemed to have taken place just yesterday.

"Maddy? You okay?"

Her face had been pressed into Noah's shoulder as the memories wreaked havoc with her mind. So she pulled herself together and pushed upright, subtly swiping at the surprising dampness on her face. "Yes. Excuse me for a moment." She rose to her feet and headed into the privacy of her room.

Matt would surely be there any minute. There was no reason to panic.

As if on cue, twin headlights flashed brightly against the window as a vehicle pulled into a parking spot near her room. She took a step toward her door when Noah rushed forward, intercepting her.

"Stay back," he ordered, flattening himself against the wall while keeping his gun pointed at the ceiling. "Take cover in the bathroom until I can verify the driver's identity."

She didn't like hiding in the bathroom but did as he asked, closing and locking the bathroom door behind her.

The seconds ticked by with infinite slowness. Even with her ear pressed to the crack of the door, she couldn't hear much of anything. Her chest tightened with fear as she imagined the motel room door being kicked in by an intruder with a gun.

Noah was armed, too, and wore a vest, but that didn't settle her heart rate.

A muffled thud caused her to gasp in alarm. She put her hand on the doorknob, intending to head out to help Noah, when there was a light rapping on the bathroom door.

"Maddy? Matt's here."

The breath whooshed from her lungs and she dropped her chin to her chest in an effort to calm herself. Then she opened the door to find Noah standing there, a grim expression on his face.

"What's wrong?" she demanded, pushing past him to get to her twin. "Mom? Nan?"

Matt held up a hand. "They're fine, Maddy. The intruder didn't get very far before the police nabbed him."

"Intruder?" Her voice rose to a shriek. "Who? When? What happened?"

"They're safe," Matt repeated, gently pushing her down onto the edge of the bed. "But Duchess and I are heading back over there to spend the night. Michael will be here any moment to pick us up. I brought a black truck for you to use."

The room spun dizzily for a moment, then centered. "Good, that's good. You and the rest of the guys should take turns being there, so they're never left alone."

"Miles will pitch in, but he and Marc have their own families to worry about, too."

"Okay, I agree we wouldn't want Miles and Marc to put their children in danger, but that still leaves you, Mitch and Mike to watch over them." She drilled him with a steely glare. "I mean it, Matt, Mom and Nan need twenty-four-seven protection until the trial is over and you know that the MPD doesn't have the manpower to do it, especially since they're not direct witnesses in the case."

"I know." The fact that her twin didn't argue made her realize he'd been shaken by the news of the intruder, too. "The police are questioning the guy who tried to get inside.

Thankfully their alarm system went off and there was a squad nearby. The perp's name is Ervin Slotterback, and he's a known drug user. It's possible he randomly chose their house because he needed a fix."

"No way. Surely you don't believe that?"

"I informed the officers that you were assaulted and that our mother and grandmother were threatened, so now they want to interview you, too."

"Not happening," Noah said bluntly. "Not until we know who to trust."

"Not tonight," Matt agreed. "Tomorrow is soon enough. Here's the key to a black 4x4 truck. Figured you may need something decent to navigate the winter roads. And it belongs to the married sister of a friend of mine, so it won't be easily linked to the Callahan name."

Noah took the key. "Thanks."

There was a second knock at the door, and this time, Maddy stayed where she was, watching as her brother Mike stepped in. The three men spoke for a moment, then Mike came over to crouch beside her. "You hanging in there?"

"Yes, and I'll be even better knowing that you're all watching over Mom and Nan." She gave her brother a quick hug. "Thanks."

Mike nodded, then turned and gestured for Matt to follow him out. She heard the roar of a car engine, then they were gone.

"It's late," Noah said. "We should get some sleep."

Maddy wanted nothing more, but she stubbornly shook her head. "No, we're going to check out Arvani's cabin first."

"Maddy, it's dark and there's no reason to charge over there right this minute—"

"Yes, there is," she interrupted, jumping to her feet. "You

don't believe a random drug addict picked my mother's house to break into any more than I do. We're running out of time. We need to do this."

Noah sighed and rubbed his palms over his face. "Okay, but put the vest on beneath your sweatshirt first. Then we'll go."

She hadn't even noticed the bulletproof vest one of her brothers must have brought in for her. Pulling it off the chair, she carried it into the bathroom and managed to get it fastened around her torso. It seemed bulky and awkward, but that couldn't be helped.

Noah was ready to go when she emerged from the bathroom. Wordlessly, she followed him outside to the four-wheel-drive black pickup. He opened the passenger door for her, then had to help her up as the vest made it difficult to maneuver.

The traffic was busy in town, but became sparse as they left the city limits. The headlights aggravated her headache, so she closed her eyes against the glare.

She must have fallen asleep because the next thing she knew, Noah was softly calling her name. "Maddy? Are you okay?"

"Fine," she murmured, wincing and rubbing the crick in her neck. They were parked at the end of a driveway marked with the numbers that matched Arvani's address. "We're here? This is Arvani's place?"

"Yeah, you slept the entire way." Noah's white teeth flashed in a smile through the darkness. "I'm glad you were able to get some rest."

"Me, too." She cleared her throat, embarrassed at the thought of Noah watching her sleep. Hopefully she hadn't drooled all over herself. "Any sign that someone has been here?"

"Yes, within the past few days. See the tire tracks in the

snow?" He gestured at the driveway that stretched out in front of them. "Today is Tuesday, well, almost Wednesday now. The last snowfall was Sunday night."

She tried not to get too excited. "Should we go in on foot?"

"Give me a minute to make sure there aren't lights on at the cabin, okay?"

She hesitated, then nodded. "Hurry up, and make sure you come back to get me. I want to go in with you."

"Understood." Noah fiddled with the bulb in the light above their seats before opening his car door. The interior stayed dark. He shut the door and quickly made his way through the wooded area surrounding the driveway.

Her breath fogged up the windows, so she wiped a spot on the glass so she could see. In a flash, Noah disappeared from view, and for a long second she felt horribly alone.

She shook it off, knowing Noah wouldn't leave her, at least not voluntarily. He was scouting out the territory, that was all. And if she couldn't see him, probably no one else could, either.

He returned surprisingly quickly, crossing over to open her door.

"Well?" she asked.

"The windows are dark. He's either asleep or gone. Let's go."

She took Noah's hand, jumping lightly down to the ground. The night air was cold but between the fleece and the vest, she was amazingly warm. Noah led her down the driveway this time, stepping carefully so as not to leave tracks so she did her best to place her feet in the exact same place.

Focused on the ground, she didn't realize Noah had stopped until she bumped into him. "What's wrong?" she whispered.

"Look." Noah pointed at dark spots staining the snow. "What is it? Oil from a car engine?"

He shook his head and pulled a slender flashlight from his utility belt. Once he aimed the light on the spots, she could see a bit more clearly. No, the spots weren't black like oil.

She swallowed hard, dragging her gaze up to meet his. The spots were a dark rust color.

Like blood.

TEN

"Is that—blood?" Maddy asked, her eyes wide and bright in the darkness.

He nodded, honestly surprised that they'd found anything useful. "Yeah, I think so. We'll take a sample to be sure."

Maddy opened her mouth, closed it, frowned, then tried again. "Whose blood?"

He pulled a slender tube from his utility belt and twisted it open, then dabbed the cotton-tipped end on the mahogany stain. This was the first break in the case and he could barely contain his relief. Finally, something to go on. "The tire tracks look to be similar to what's on our vehicle, a sixteen-inch truck tire. If the truck had been backed into the driveway, these bloodstains would have come from the passenger-side door."

"Jackson." Her fingers clutched his arm. "You think this is evidence of Arvani shoving Jackson into the passenger seat after the murder."

Noah slipped the vial back in his pocket and turned off the flashlight, hoping, praying this was the clue he needed to prove his innocence. "We'll know more once we get this blood tested in the lab, but yeah. That's exactly what I think. It's the only thing that makes sense. Even if the cops wanted to keep Jackson's murder quiet, they'd still have to notify his next of kin and there's no guarantee that they would keep quiet. But if Arvani got rid of the body and moved the truck, then there would be nothing to report, other than a missing person."

Like the prosecutor she was, Maddy immediately picked up on his train of thought. "And missing adults don't make headlines until they've been gone for an extended period of time. Or unless someone within the family creates a ruckus."

"Exactly. I don't remember Jackson's schedule. Sometimes he took odd days off and if he had, there would be no reason for the police to raise an alarm." He swept his gaze over the area. There was a long stack of chopped wood neatly piled up between two large oak trees off to the right of the cabin. The patches of snow covering the ground were large enough that if they took a direct route up to the cabin, they risked leaving footprints. Yet he really wanted to take a look inside to see if there were additional signs that someone had been inside recently. The tire tracks were good, but they could belong to anyone, even someone driving in by mistake.

Maybe if they went around through the trees, coming in from the side of the house closest to the woods? If Arvani had been here in the past few days, he would have left tracks between the cabin and the woodpile.

"Now what?" Maddy asked, breaking into his thoughts.

"This way." He turned, moving slowly so that he could be sure not to leave footprints. Maddy once again gripped the back of his utility belt, following close, making him smile.

He didn't like knowing Maddy's mother and grandmother were in danger, yet being with Maddy like this, working the case with her, was no hardship. Noah hadn't experienced this kind of connection since working alongside Matt.

He reminded himself that this was only a temporary arrangement. After Arvani's trial, he and Maddy would go their separate ways.

Depressing thought.

The process was slow, and he hoped that they weren't caught in the act by Lance Arvani's return. The moon was bright in the sky, illuminating the patches of snow. When he finally reached the woodpile, he was disappointed to see there were no footprints between the front door of the cabin and the pile of logs.

Was it possible Arvani hadn't been staying here? Or had he given the key to his cabin to someone else? That didn't seem likely without any footprints leading to the woodpile.

The balloon of euphoria he'd experienced at seeing the blood in the driveway instantly deflated. So what if he was able to prove the blood belonged to Jackson? The link to Arvani was slim.

"What's wrong?" Maddy whispered.

"Nothing." He mentally measured the distance from where they were standing to the side of the cabin. There were a few bare patches, but too far apart for Maddy's shorter stride. "Do me a favor and stay here. I'm just going to take a quick peek through the window."

"Okay."

He took long, wide steps, carefully placing his feet on the parts of the ground not covered in snow. It didn't take long to reach the structure. Cupping his hands around his eyes, he peered through the window.

It wasn't easy to see much at first, but he was able to distinguish shapes. A tall dresser and a wide bed that had obviously been used recently and left unmade. His gaze stumbled across a chair with a duffel bag on it.

Someone staying here might take off for a while, but leaving a duffel bag behind indicated that person would likely return.

Arvani? Or someone else?

Using his penlight, he flashed it in the window, hoping to see through the doorway into the room beyond. He caught a glimpse of a sofa and what looked like a corner of a fireplace. He rationalized that there might be a decent stack of wood already inside the cabin, which could be why no one had come outside yet to get more.

He turned off the light and made his way back to where Maddy was waiting, huddled beside one of the large oak trees. "I believe the cabin is being used. We need to get out of here before he returns."

"Lead the way," she said, shivering in the cold.

Ignoring the sense of urgency wasn't easy, but he forced himself to go slow, unwilling to make any mistakes. After what seemed like an eternity, they reached the road. He opened the passenger-side door and assisted Maddy up into the seat. He was rounding the back of the truck when he spotted headlights on the road, a few miles in the distance.

He leaped into the driver's seat and tapped the brakes long enough to start the engine before letting up and easing on the gas. Racing away would only draw more attention, so he drove slowly at first, gradually picking up speed. He flicked the lights off, but could still see dim running lights. He searched for a way to shut them off, but couldn't find the switch, so he gave up.

Technology didn't help in situations like this.

Maddy leaned forward, turning up the heat. "That was close."

"Yeah, although there's no way to know if that vehicle back there was heading to the cabin or somewhere else."

He continued down the highway, trying to keep an eye on the headlights behind them.

The lights vanished from his field of vision as the driver turned off the highway.

Noah quickly slowed down, making a three-point turn to head back.

"What are you doing?" Maddy asked, her voice raised in alarm.

"I want to see if the car pulled into Arvani's driveway," he said. "Help me look as we drive by, okay?"

She nodded and leaned forward so she could see past him. He kept his speed steady but not too fast so they'd miss it.

"There!" Maddy said excitedly. He nodded in agreement as he caught sight of the large shape of a truck parked in front of Arvani's cabin.

He'd only gotten a quick glimpse, but he was certain the vehicle was the same one Jackson had been driving the night of his murder.

Somehow, some way, he needed to prove it.

Maddy couldn't believe they'd gotten away from Arvani's place in the nick of time. If they'd been five or ten minutes later, they would have been caught for sure.

She sent up a quick prayer of thanks to God for watching over them.

Noah slowed the vehicle and turned. The truck bobbed up and down as he went down through the shallow ditch up the embankment and then through a small clearing.

"You're not seriously going back there, are you?" she asked when he threw the gearshift into Park.

"Yeah, just long enough to get the license plate number." He shut down the engine and handed her the keys. "Will you be warm enough for a few minutes?"

"Sure." The word was barely out of her mouth when he pushed open the driver-side door and jumped out, slamming it shut behind him.

Truthfully she didn't like it, but tagging along would only increase the risk of Noah's being seen, so she huddled down in the seat and waited.

Three minutes passed, and she told herself not to worry. Noah wouldn't be rushing down to Arvani's driveway, he'd be moving slowly, taking his time. After five minutes, she twisted around in her seat to look out through the rear window, trying to see if Noah was on his way back.

Seven minutes later, her heart rate sped up with distress. What if something had happened to him? Arvani could have caught Noah sneaking around the edge of his property.

Ten minutes was more than enough. She needed to take action. Scrambling over the middle console, she adjusted the seat for her shorter legs and started the engine. She'd never driven a truck this big, but since there was nothing but trees and brush on either side, she figured she couldn't do much harm.

After putting the truck in Reverse, she drew a deep breath and slowly rolled backward out of the woods. The rear end of the truck tipped downward, scraping along the ground, making her wince.

A loud banging on the side of the truck had her slamming on the brakes, her heart lodged into her throat. Then Noah's face was pressed against her window.

He was all right!

She threw the truck back into Park and unlocked the door. Noah opened it and she made room for him to get inside by scrambling back into her own seat.

"What took you so long?" she demanded. "I was going crazy waiting here for you."

"I know. I hung back, making sure the guy was inside the cabin before creeping close enough to see the license plate."

"And?" she asked, as he maneuvered the truck back out to the highway.

He headed back the way they'd originally come, toward the interstate that would take them to Milwaukee. "The tag number is 555 EVP."

She repeated the series of numbers and letters to herself, committing it to memory. "Does it belong to Jackson?"

"Same make and model, but I don't know his plate number off the top of my head. I'll check with the DMV records when we get back to the motel."

She nodded, knowing cops had access to the DMV database. Even her brother Michael, who worked as a private investigator, had that capability. Several DAs used private investigators to help them find witnesses that might not want to be found, and her brother was just one of the PIs taking on the occasional case for them.

Thinking of her brother reminded her of the intruder who had been caught outside her mom's house. She knew the guy had to have been sent by Pietro's goons, but why would they send someone so low on the criminal totem pole? The guy who'd assaulted her outside the courthouse and rammed them into Lake Michigan hadn't been some low-life drug addict.

What had Matt said the intruder's name was? Slotterback? Yeah, that was it. Ervin Slotterback.

Maybe Pietro had sent him as a scare tactic. To prove he could get to her mom and Nan if he really wanted to. She swallowed hard, reminding herself that Matt and Duchess would take good care of them.

"Are you hungry?" Noah asked, breaking the silence. "I can pick something up on the way back to the motel."

The late lunch they'd eaten prior to meeting up with her twin seemed ages ago. Fast food wasn't her favorite, but it was better than nothing. "Now that you mention it, I could eat. It's pretty late, though, most places won't be open."

"I know. We'll have to settle for a burger."

She wrinkled her nose. "See if there's a salad."

Noah waited until they were closer to the motel before pulling into a fast-food restaurant. They used the drive-through and were back on the road in no time.

She'd given up meat, but the fries still smelled good. Noah pulled into the parking lot of their motel, a place called The American Lodge, and backed into the parking spot so they could drive out in a hurry if needed.

She followed him into his room and waited for him to set up the computer. The vest was heavy beneath her fleece and she toyed with the idea of taking it off, but then decided to wait for a bit.

Noah quickly logged in to the computer. She watched over his shoulder as he brought up the DMV database and punched in his username and password. When he entered the license plate number, the program's icon spun in a circle as it searched for the information.

She began to unpack their food as he stared at the screen. Suddenly a new page bloomed into view.

"I knew it," Noah said with satisfaction. He tapped at the screen. "The license plate belongs to my partner, Jackson S. Dellis." He turned to look up at her. "Arvani is linked to Pietro and to my partner's death. I'm convinced now, and the blood I found at the scene will prove it."

She gave him a hug. "I'm so glad. We'll get to the bottom of this yet. Now, do you mind if we eat? I'm famished."

"Yeah, sure." He pushed the computer off to the side, making room.

Maddy finished unpacking the meal, then took her seat.

Noah dropped down beside her. She glanced at him from beneath her lashes, wondering if he'd initiate the prayer.

He did. Clearing his throat, he began, "Dear Lord, bless this food we are about to eat and, um, keep us safe as we seek to bring a murderer to justice. Amen."

"Amen," she echoed. She smiled and reached out to lightly clasp his hand. "That was nice, Noah, thank you."

He ducked his head as if embarrassed. "Thanks, but to be honest I don't know much about praying, other than what I learned at the Callahan family meals."

"Oh, Noah." She ached to throw herself into his arms. "You're always welcome to join us at church services and at brunch. You know very well Mom and Nan make enough food to feed an army."

He took a bite of his burger, then gave her a sideways glance. "I didn't feel welcome, not after Matt's injury."

She grimaced with shame. "I'm sorry. I know that was my fault. I should never have blamed you for Matt's stab wound. I know, better than most, that police officers put their lives on the line every single day."

She thought for a moment about how her father, former police chief Max Callahan, had been shot in the line of duty. In her spare time, which truthfully hadn't been very often since the Pietro case had been dropped in her lap, she pored over the police reports related to her father's shooting, trying to find some clue the homicide detectives had missed. It irked her that his murder still hadn't been solved and deep down she thought part of the reason was that the mayor had refused to let her brother Miles participate in the investigation, claiming he was too close to the victim to be objective.

Now almost two years had passed. The colder the case, the less likely it was they would find the perpetrator responsible.

Not that she planned to give up. Once the Pietro case was finished, she planned on taking some well-deserved vacation time to continue her own investigation. She kept the file related to their dad's murder hidden in her desk.

They ate in silence for several moments, enjoying the meal. When they were almost finished, Noah sat back in his seat with a heavy sigh. "You were right to blame me for Matt's injury," he said in a blunt tone.

"No, I wasn't." She stole one of his french fries and popped it in her mouth, chewing thoughtfully. "I actually saw the case file, you know. I'm the one who brought charges against the woman responsible. A drug addict named Corrine Lobely stabbed Matt, not you. It wasn't fair of me to insinuate otherwise."

Noah pushed the remnants of his meal away. "I hesitated just for a split second, but it was long enough for her to cut him. So just know I've been blaming myself, too."

She hated knowing that he carried that guilt, along with feeling responsible for his college girlfriend's death. "Noah, cops often have to make split-second decisions. Life-and-death decisions. Playing Monday-morning quarterback is easy, but not realistic. I don't blame you at all. In fact, it's hard to blame Corrine."

Noah's gaze snapped up to meet hers. "What do you mean? Of course she's guilty."

She munched another fry. "Yes, she's guilty of a crime, that's true. But I said it's hard to blame her. Do you know her background? She was raised in the foster system, physically abused and shuffled from one house to another. At the time she stabbed Matt, she'd been living out on the street for six months after being aged out of the foster-care system." Corrine's case file had been difficult to read, each word seared into her brain. "Who's to say that couldn't have been me, or one of my brothers, if we hadn't been fortunate enough to have been born into the Callahan family?"

Noah dropped his gaze. "Not all kids from broken homes end up drug addicts, and some kids who have decent families can still get caught up with drugs."

She sensed he was talking about something personal, and wanted to pry, but forced herself to hold back.

"Regardless, Matt blames me, too," Noah continued. "Sure, he claimed that he'd always wanted to be a K-9 cop, but the fact that he went straight into training immediately after the incident tells me that the truth is simply that he didn't trust me anymore. And I can't say that I really blame him."

She turned and took Noah's hand in hers. "That's not true. In fact, Matt was the one who convinced me to forgive you the way Jesus taught us. He held me responsible for you not coming over anymore. Trust me, Matt misses you. The two of you were more than just partners. You were friends."

His brown eyes held a hint of hope. "He really said that?"

"Absolutely. So promise me that once we finish this case, you'll come to church and brunch again."

The corner of his mouth tipped up in a lopsided smile. "How can I turn down an invitation like that?"

"Yes! I'm so happy." Impulsively, she leaned forward and kissed him on the cheek. Noah put his arm around her and held her close for a moment, then he turned his head and their lips met. Clung. Deepened into a toe-curling kiss.

This time, he initiated the embrace and she willingly kissed him back, marveling in the fact that Noah had managed to break through the fear that had held her captive for far too long.

ELEVEN

Kissing Maddy hadn't been a part of his plan, but she tasted so sweet he couldn't help himself. How long had it been since he'd kissed a woman? Too long. Years, even.

Maddy broke off from their kiss. But she didn't step away; instead she snuggled against him, her palm spread over his heart.

"I feel so safe with you, Noah," she said in a low voice.

Safe? Gina's pretty face and delicate features flashed in his mind and he felt as if someone had smashed a fist into his gut.

Safe? He didn't do relationships, and even if he wanted to try again, there was no guarantee things would work out for them.

Safe? He'd protect Maddy with his life, but emotionally? Nope, he didn't see how he could accomplish that.

She must have sensed his distress because she pulled away, looking up at him with concern mirrored in her clear blue eyes. "What is it?"

"Dangerous situations often create a false sense of intimacy," he said, pushing the words past his tight throat. "I'm glad you feel safe with me, Maddy, but we can't read too much into these feelings."

Her frown deepened. "Don't tell me about how I'm feeling, Noah."

The hurt lacing her tone only made him feel worse. His past experiences with his sister and Gina weren't her fault. "I just don't want you to say something you'll regret later, once the danger has passed and your life has returned to normal."

Her laugh was bitter as she abruptly pulled away. "You don't know anything about what I've been through, Noah. Thanks for showing me I can still be near a man without feeling sick to my stomach. I appreciate it."

Her words were like a slap across the face. His hand flailed out, trying to capture hers, but she was already halfway across the room, heading for the connecting door. "What do you mean?" he demanded harshly, moving quickly to catch up with her. "Why would you feel sick? What happened? Did someone hurt you?"

"Good night, Noah." Maddy stepped over the threshold before he could stop her, and she closed her side of the door. There was an audible click as she shot the dead bolt home.

He stared at the door mere inches from his face, his thoughts whirling. Maddy had given him a glimpse at something he'd never imagined. Some guy must have hurt her, but how was that possible? No one would be brave enough to mess with the Callahans, and everyone knew that Maddy was the youngest of six with five older brothers. Any guy daring to hurt her would have to face all of them. Especially her twin.

Wouldn't they?

Unless— He tipped his head down, resting his forehead on the cool, flat surface of the door, his chaotic thoughts torturous now. Unless she hadn't told her brothers, in some weird attempt to protect them from acting crazy on her behalf.

The minute the thought formed in his mind, he knew he'd hit the nail squarely on the head. Her brothers were all involved in some sort of law enforcement, except for Mike, who was a private investigator, one who did some work for the DA's office. Of course she wouldn't want them to risk doing something that might hurt their careers.

So she'd held her silence. Until now.

He let out a low groan, knowing he'd handled that badly. He should have been understanding, gently encouraging her to open up.

Instead he'd chased her away.

And now she'd locked herself in her room.

Idiot. He was a complete and total idiot. But there was nothing more he could do now. Maybe in the morning she'd be more willing to accept his apology.

He turned away from the connecting doorway and stared blindly at Maddy's computer. Showed how upset she was that she'd left it behind. Exhaustion pulled at him, but he thrust it aside and sat down to continue their investigation. Since Jackson's murder hadn't hit the news, and his partner's truck was temporarily parked in Arvani's driveway, maybe Noah wasn't a current murder suspect after all.

It was time to reach out to his boss, Lieutenant Allan O'Grady. For one thing, he had proof that Jackson's murder wasn't his fault. But the bigger issue is that Maddy would need to go into the police station in the morning to give her statement anyway, so it made sense for him to let his superiors know what was going on, as well. Still, he didn't want to call the precinct again from his disposable phone. He logged in to his work email and sent a brief message.

Sorry I've been AWOL, but my squad car ending up in the lake was no accident. There have also been several attempts on ADA Madison Callahan's life. I've been keeping her safe, but I'd like to meet with you in the morning to discuss next steps.
Thanks, Officer Noah Sinclair.

He reviewed his message before clicking the send button. Because of the late hour, just past midnight, he didn't expect a response, but one popped up almost immediately.

Be in my office at 0900 sharp.

The message didn't sound encouraging. In fact, Noah suspected that if he didn't show up as ordered, he needn't bother coming in at all. He let out a sigh, shut down the computer and forced himself to stretch out on the bed.

Sleep was essential before facing off with his boss in the morning. Oddly enough, his last thought was that he wasn't nearly as worried about maintaining his job as he was about keeping Maddy safe.

Despite her bone-deep weariness, Maddy tossed and turned for the next hour, unable to sleep. She regretted giving Noah even a hint as to what Blake had done. No doubt he'd grill Matt for more information, which wouldn't help as she hadn't said a word about Ratcliff to anyone.

Especially not Matt.

Growing up with five brothers hadn't been easy. They scared off more boyfriends than she could count. They'd also taken a very personal interest in teaching her how to defend herself. She knew how to fight off an attack, but when Blake had pinned her against the desk, she'd somehow missed his true intent until it was too late.

Stupid? Maybe. The fact of the matter was that Blake had been her colleague, another ADA. A lawyer! Why would she suspect he'd stoop so low as to use force against her?

The bite of shame lingered, and she did her best to put it out of her mind. Blake wasn't important; her case against Pietro was.

Noah? Well, it was her own fault for allowing him to become a distraction. He'd been clear from the beginning he wasn't interested in a relationship, so she needed to get over it already.

Two kisses in the grand scheme of things meant nothing. He was a nice guy who'd made it his mission to keep her safe.

But he was also the man who wasn't used to praying. Who'd made it clear everything he'd learned about faith had come from spending time with her family. She couldn't, wouldn't let him flounder on his own. She'd meant it when she'd invited him over for church services and brunch. Maybe even for the Christmas holiday.

So that settled it, then. She and Noah would be friends. Nothing more, nothing less.

She ignored the tiny hollow place in her heart and prayed for sleep to come.

Her internal body clock woke her up at six in the morning. With a moan, she rolled out of bed and padded to the bathroom. A nice hot shower made her feel more human, as did blow-drying her hair. Although looking at the clothes she'd been wearing—for what, two days now?—had her wrinkling her nose in disgust. Ick. No way was she wearing those to the police station, or worse, to her office.

She'd ask Noah to stop at her place for fresh things before going in to give her statement. It would be cheaper than wasting their cash reserves on new clothes.

Thumps and bumps from next door convinced her that Noah was up and about, too. Squaring her shoulders, she crossed over and twisted the dead bolt off. She opened her side an inch or so, then returned to packing her meager belongings together. She set the bulletproof vest aside. She wouldn't wear the fleece sweater to give her statement, and the vest wouldn't fit beneath her business clothes.

"Maddy?" Noah rapped lightly on the door. "You decent?"

She felt her cheeks warm, and inwardly bemoaned her fair skin. "Yes, of course."

Noah pushed open the door and hovered at the threshold, his gaze serious. "I'm sorry for upsetting you last night."

She shrugged and turned away to place the folded fleece sweatshirt he'd purchased for her in the plastic bag. "I'm fine. Let's just forget about that for now. We need a game plan. I thought we could grab something to eat and review how much you want me to tell the police when I provide my statement."

That made him frown. "What are you talking about? You should tell them everything."

She raised her head, looking him directly in the eye. "You want me to tell them we watched your partner die from a gunshot wound before our eyes? But oh, by the way there's no dead body? What if they decide to hold you for further questioning?"

He grimaced and shrugged. "I don't want you to lie for me, Maddy. Besides, I've been ordered in to talk to my lieutenant as well, at nine sharp. The entire truth will come out sooner or later."

Panic squeezed her chest. She stepped closer, her gaze beseeching him to listen. "Please, Noah. Let's talk about this over breakfast. We don't have to lie, but we don't have to tell them everything right away, do we? Can't we give them what we know about Pietro's attempt to get me off the case by threatening my family and leave it at that?"

His gaze was troubled. "I have to explain about how we were followed and rear-ended into Lake Michigan. And how we were shot at while escaping into the boat that was left unattended at the dock. The boat owner deserves a replacement."

"That's reasonable," she agreed. "But what about the blood we found in the driveway of Arvani's cabin? How are we going to get that tested without mentioning Jackson?"

He hesitated, then shrugged. "I don't know. Give me some time to think about it. If you were serious about getting breakfast, we should leave now."

"Okay." She reached for the bag, but Noah beat her to it, taking both the bag and the spare vest. "But I also need to stop at my place for a change of clothes. I can't go into the office looking like this."

"I'd rather you didn't go in at all," Noah muttered. He stood to the side, allowing her to go through first. "Let's hope it's less risky to go in the daylight."

She understood where he was coming from, and truthfully, she didn't want to put Noah in any more danger, either. But appearance was important while preparing witnesses, more so for her as one of the few female ADAs. She needed to look confident, secure in her knowledge and ability to uphold the law.

Fully capable of convincing a jury to put Alexander Pietro away for the rest of his life.

Noah stored their things, including her computer case, in the narrow area behind the front seat of the truck. He drove to a family-style restaurant that served breakfast all day.

Their server poured coffee and brought their meals with record-breaking speed, but this time, Noah simply bowed his head, waiting for Maddy to say the blessing.

"Dear Lord, thank You for providing this food we are about to eat. Please continue to show us the way, following Your chosen path. We ask for Your care and guidance as we seek to bring criminals to justice. Amen."

There was a slight pause before Noah added, "Amen."

"Dig in," she said in a light, playful tone. It was customary for one of the Callahan boys to utter those words after saying grace, making everyone laugh.

Noah's mouth quirked in a smile. "The first time I had dinner at your house and heard Matt say that, I thought your mother was going to yell at him."

"No, she wouldn't do that," Maddy said, taking a bite of her scrambled eggs. "Even my father, who was always the disciplinarian in the household, didn't raise his voice to us very often. Trust me, his disappointment was punishment enough."

Noah nodded but didn't say anything more, focusing instead on his meal.

She couldn't help wondering about his family. She thought back to the few times they'd eaten together. He'd laughed and joked with the rest of them, but hadn't said much about his parents or siblings. She knew he wasn't an only child. Matt had mentioned that Noah had a younger sister and an older brother.

Matt had been born a full three minutes before her, a fact he gloated over incessantly. As if three minutes meant anything. Not hardly.

Despite the overbearing nature of her brothers, Maddy secretly admitted she wouldn't trade them for anything.

"What if we stopped at a department store instead of going to your condo?" Noah asked, breaking into her thoughts.

She shook her head. "Waste of money. We'll be safe enough during the day, won't we? I'm sure we can get in and out before anyone notices."

"Unless Pietro's goons have someone watching the place," Noah countered. "Matt provided plenty of cash and the stores are open early for the Christmas rush."

She didn't like it but sensed there was no point in arguing. "Fine, my favorite department store isn't far from here. We'll stop there, okay?"

"Sounds good," Noah said, with such obvious relief that she instantly felt bad. The night of her attack seemed like a long time ago, but it really wasn't.

And she knew deep down Noah was still worried about her safety.

They finished their meal, then headed to the store. She found a pair of navy blue dress slacks with a matching blazer and paired them up with a crisp white blouse. After purchasing the items, she changed in the restroom.

"You look great, Maddy," Noah said when she emerged. "Ready to give your statement?"

"I am." When they were back out in the truck, she turned to face him. "I've decided to tell the police everything up until Jackson's murder, especially since we know the body has been moved. I don't want to give them a reason to consider you a suspect."

"A lie of omission is still a lie. As an officer of the court, you're sworn to uphold the law."

She winced, knowing he was right. "I understand that, but how can we protect you?"

He reached out to cover her hand with his. "We were both there, Maddy. Two witnesses to a crime. We need to be honest and tell them everything. I'll provide the blood sample we found and request for it to be tested. Getting a positive ID on the blood will add more credibility to our case."

She closed her eyes for a moment, then nodded. "Okay. If you're sure."

"I am. But the one caveat here is that we're both going to speak only to my lieutenant. No one else."

She was relieved to hear it. "I'm on board with that plan."

Noah drove directly to the Fifth District police station parking lot. He led the way inside to Lieutenant O'Grady's office with ten minutes to spare. They were told to wait, and O'Grady opened the door at exactly nine o'clock to let them in.

The lieutenant appeared to be in his early fifties; he had dark hair with a touch of silvery gray at his temples and piercing green eyes. His expression remained neutral as Noah introduced her, and he urged her to start at the beginning.

Maddy explained about leaving the courthouse late on Monday night, being held at knifepoint, the scar on her neck evidence of the blade cutting her skin. She told the entire story, all the way through, without interruption.

When she finished, the lieutenant turned to Noah. "You're sure the person you witnessed being shot was your partner, Jackson Dellis?"

"Yes, sir," Noah answered. "I called him for a ride and distinctly remember seeing his red hair."

O'Grady stroked his chin, his gaze thoughtful. "That's quite a story."

Maddy's face flushed with anger and it wasn't easy to keep her tone level. "It's not a story, it's the truth. I was threatened and shot at. My family was threatened, too.

The police caught a guy by the name of Ervin Slotterback trying to get into my mother's house. Pietro is getting desperate, willing to do whatever he deems necessary to derail this trial."

"Okay, I can buy that part," O'Grady said with a drawn-out sigh. "But witnessing a murder when there's no body or other evidence of a crime? That's pushing it."

"Sir, we have reason to believe a Chicago cop by the name of Lance Arvani is involved with Pietro's narcotic trafficking business. He owns a cabin near Willow Lake, Wisconsin, and we took a sample of blood that we found on his driveway." Noah pulled the vial out of his pocket. "I request that this be tested to see if it's a DNA match for Officer Dellis. Jackson's truck was in Arvani's driveway, as well. That and the blood should be more than enough to obtain a search warrant."

O'Grady leaned back in his seat and crossed his arms across his chest. "Okay, fine. Take the blood down to the lab and write up your search warrant. If the blood type matches Dellis, I'm sure we'll find a judge to sign off on the warrant."

Maddy wanted to point out that by then, Arvani could be long gone, but she bit her tongue. She should be used to this sort of delay by now. The wheels of justice never moved as quickly as she and the police would like.

"Thank you, sir." Noah replaced the vial in his pocket and rose to his feet. "With your permission, I'd like to escort ADA Callahan to her office and stand guard as she continues to prepare for trial."

O'Grady's eyebrows levered up, but then he nodded and also stood. He held his hand out to Maddy. "It was nice to meet you, Ms. Callahan. I respected your father's leadership over this department very much."

She shook his hand. "Thank you. I appreciate you freeing up Officer Sinclair from his usual duties in order to provide me assistance."

"Not a problem." The words were polite, but the scowl on his face made her think that the lieutenant didn't relish the thought of telling his boss what he'd just agreed to.

Noah held the door open for her. They walked through the police station and were almost to the door before she heard Noah's name.

"Sinclair! Wait up!"

Noah made a frustrated sound but turned to look at the officer who'd flagged them down. "What is it?"

"The call just came in about an explosion. The address is a building housing several condos." The officer glanced at her. "ADA Callahan's building."

Maddy gasped, blood draining from her face as the news hit hard. Her building? She gripped Noah's arm tightly. "We need to go over there right away."

"No way, Maddy. It's too dangerous."

She gave his arm a little shake. "I don't care! I need to know that Gretchen is okay."

He reluctantly nodded and escorted her outside toward the truck.

She curled her fingers into fists, hoping and praying that Gretchen was all right. That it hadn't been her roommate returning home from her job as a flight assistant that had somehow triggered the blast.

A bomb potentially meant for Maddy.

TWELVE

The last thing Noah wanted was to take Maddy to her condo, but he didn't know how to talk her out of it. He understood being afraid that her roommate might have been in the building, but going there wouldn't change anything. With the firefighters working the scene, it would be hours before they'd get any specific information.

Days, even.

He helped her into the truck, then slid in behind the wheel. After he pulled into traffic, he handed his disposable phone to Maddy. "Do you know Gretchen's number?"

She thought for a moment, then nodded, punching in the numbers. Her expression was full of hope at first, but as the ringing continued without an answer, it drained from her face.

"Gretchen? It's Maddy. Please call me at this number as soon as possible. It's urgent. You might be in danger." She disconnected from the call but kept the phone clutched in her hand.

"Do you remember her schedule?"

She shook her head, staring grimly out the passenger-side window. "No. It's always changing. At first she used to call me when flights were running late, but not anymore."

He sensed her despair. "This isn't your fault," he reminded her.

"Isn't it? I should have anticipated something like this. I should have tried to get in touch with Gretchen to warn her about the danger!" Maddy's voice was low and full of anguish.

"Then blame me. You didn't even remember you had a roommate after your head injury."

She shook her head, then rested her forehead against the foggy glass. "My memory has been back since late yesterday afternoon."

"And I could have warned her before that," he reiterated.

She turned and reached for his hand. Then she bowed her head. "Dear Lord, please keep Gretchen safe in Your care."

"Amen," Noah added. He continued to hold her hand, hating feeling so helpless. He wished he had thought about calling Gretchen, but his priority had been keeping Maddy safe.

And he'd be lying if he didn't admit it still was.

It was no surprise to find the roads leading to Maddy's building were closed off. He pulled over to the side of the street, then shut off the engine. "We'll have to walk from here."

"I know." Maddy didn't wait for his help but pushed open the door and jumped down. He swept his gaze over the area as he came around to join her. Placing a protective arm around her shoulders, he kept himself positioned between her and the street.

It probably wasn't a trap, but he refused to let his guard down just in case. They'd taken only a few steps before they were approached by two officers.

"I'm sorry, but we can't let you through," the female officer said. Noah didn't know her name, but her name badge identified her last name as Rapine. "This area is a crime scene."

"I'm Officer Sinclair and this is ADA Callahan. She lives here. What can you tell us about what happened?"

The two patrol officers glanced at each other, then Rapine shrugged. "All I know is the call about an explosion came in around zero eight hundred hours. The smoke eaters are working on dousing the blaze now."

"What about the occupants of the building?" Maddy asked. "Did everyone get out safe?"

The two officers exchanged another uneasy glance. "Several people were evacuated. I can't tell you anything more than that."

Maddy made a soft sound of distress so he tightened his grip around her shoulders. "You must have some idea which unit was the source of the blast?"

"Somewhere on the third floor." The male officer, last name of Otto, spoke up for the first time. "But we don't have any information related to possible casualties. The scene is still too hot for that, and besides, you know that it will take time to investigate exactly what happened and to reach everyone living there."

Maddy shivered, and Noah didn't think it was from the freezing cold temperatures. "Thank you," she said to the officers.

"Not a problem," Rapine said. "We'll note for the record that you weren't home when this occurred."

"Will you please continue to try to reach Gretchen Herald? She's my roommate. I own the condo, but she lives there with me."

Otto nodded and took out his notebook. "Sure."

"I'd like to get closer," Maddy added.

Rapine shook her head. "I'm sorry, but we can't allow

that. There's really nothing to see other than the firefighters working the blaze."

"Come on, Maddy. There's nothing more we can do here." Noah agreed with the officers that seeing the condo building on fire wasn't going to help her cope.

The only thing that would make her feel better was to hear from Gretchen.

Maddy reluctantly nodded, allowing him to escort her back to the truck he'd accidentally left illegally parked in front of a fire hydrant.

"Please take me to my office," Maddy begged, once they were settled inside the vehicle. "I need to work this case."

He swallowed a sigh. "Okay, but I don't want to take you in the main entrance. Is there another way to get in that's more private? Less risk of being seen?"

"Yes. We can go in the back way. Park in the courthouse parking lot and I'll show you where to go."

Parking for the Milwaukee County courthouse was in an underground structure, not ideal by any means, but there would also be plenty of other cars down there so they could easily blend in. Still, Noah felt as if they were a bit vulnerable as he pulled in and headed down the long concrete driveway, winding down and around until he found open parking spaces.

"Try to find a spot over toward the stairwell in the corner," Maddy instructed.

He did as she requested, getting as close as he could. The stairwell was also lined in concrete walls and had steel railings. Even at ten fifteen in the morning, there were still plenty of people, many of whom were lawyers, heading toward the elevator adjacent to the stairway.

Maddy led the way, which was okay with him since he preferred covering her back. He'd feel better if she was armed or wearing the vest, but as she mentioned before, the courthouse and DA's office building should be safe.

But even though there were sheriff's deputies manning the entrances and exits of the courthouse, there wasn't nearly that level of security for the DA's offices.

When Maddy reached the top of the stairs, she turned right, heading in the opposite direction of the courthouse. The cold air nipped the tips of his ears but he followed Maddy along the narrow walkway to an inconspicuous doorway at the side of the Milwaukee County Government building.

"Isn't it locked?" he asked as Maddy approached.

She nodded. "Good thing this wasn't in my purse, either." She drew her badge from the depths of her coat pocket and pressed it against a black square electronic reader. The door buzzed and he quickly pulled it open.

The offices here were small and cramped, not that the ADA offices were much bigger. He assumed these were lower level government staff members working in this area.

When Maddy turned a corner, the main corridor for the ADA offices came into view. As they walked past, most of the people nodded or greeted Maddy by name. He was surprised that so far, no one acted as if they knew she hadn't been there in well over twenty-four hours.

Maddy opened a door and entered a large office area, with several smaller offices on the left and the most senior ADA's office, belonging to Jarrod Fine, on the right. His door was open and the minute he caught sight of Maddy, he bellowed, "Callahan! Where have you been?"

"Hi, Jarrod, what's wrong? Did you miss me?" Maddy moved toward her office, but Fine leaped to his feet, nearly displacing his badly fitting toupee.

"In my office, now!"

"Okay." Maddy didn't look at all flustered as she opened her door, took off her coat and draped it over a chair. "Have a seat, Noah. This could take a while."

He stood watching, feeling awkward as she disappeared into Fine's office, the door closing softly behind her.

Dropping into the chair next to her desk, he stared at the closed door, not liking the fact that she was out of his line of sight. In fact, he didn't like being this far away from her, period.

What if Fine was the man who'd tried to hurt her? His stomach knotted, but then he shook his head. Doing something like that didn't seem to be Jarrod Fine's style.

He drew in a deep breath and scrubbed his hands over his face. Frankly, none of this sat well with him. This was going to be a long, tedious day of playing bodyguard.

Especially considering what he really wanted to do was to investigate Jackson's murder, as well as continue digging into the attempts on Maddy's life.

The trial was five days away not counting today. Five days seemed like an eternity when it came to keeping Maddy safe.

Maddy kept her face an emotionless mask as Jarrod glared at her, every muscle in his body quivering, as did the hairpiece he insisted on wearing. "You know how important the Pietro case is, don't you? Disappearing like that without notice, not even a single phone call, was incredibly unprofessional."

"I can provide a doctor's excuse if necessary," Maddy said calmly. "And, oh, by the way, Pietro's men have tried to kill me several times and have threatened my family."

He reared back in his seat, as if shocked by the news. "What? When?"

Maddy filled him in on her attack outside the courthouse and the subsequent attempts on her life and Noah's. For once Jarrod didn't say anything but actually listened intently as she described how they'd managed to escape, not just once, but several times. She finished her story by describing the new lead they'd uncovered about Lance Arvani, the Chicago police officer with property in Wisconsin.

"We need more on Arvani," Jarrod said as if he hadn't taken her to task for being unprofessional. And of course he hadn't bothered to follow up on her offer of a doctor's excuse, either. Jarrod didn't care as much about his employees as he did about their work. She was obligated to fill him in on where she was on the case.

"The blood we found in Arvani's driveway has been sent to the lab. We're hoping to at least get a basic blood type match to Jackson Dellis because DNA will take weeks."

Fine scowled. "I'll call in some favors, see if I can get the DNA fast-tracked. We need those results."

"I'd appreciate that." This was why she put up with Fine's overbearing personality. When he wanted something done, he didn't let anything get in his way. "My plan is to continue with witness preparation, unless you have something else you need."

Her boss waved his hand. "Get to work. But next time, let me know what's going on."

"Of course." She rose to her feet. "I almost forgot to mention that there was an explosion in my condo building earlier this morning." She swallowed hard, the image of Gretchen's face with her shiny blond hair and hazel eyes making her feel sick to her stomach. Still, she forced herself to remain professional. "Number of casualties still unknown."

"Explosion?" For the first time since she'd entered his office, Jarrod actually looked upset. "Related to Pietro?"

She shrugged. "That's the working theory at the moment. The coincidence on the heels of everything that's happened over the past few days is difficult to ignore."

"Be careful, Maddy." Jarrod must have been concerned because he never, ever called her by her first name. "Alexander Pietro may be one of the most dangerous men you've ever faced across the courtroom."

"Yes, I know." She had the concussion and the bullet fragment in Noah's vest, not to mention Jackson's murder, to prove it. "Officer Sinclair is on duty to protect me." When Jarrod opened his mouth to argue, she held up a hand. "I know he's on the witness list and I'll do everything possible to minimize his exposure to the others, but frankly, it's already too late for that. He's been with me since I was first attacked and is a key witness to the attempts to harm us and to his partner's murder. So we'll just need to find a way to deal with that while maintaining the integrity of the case."

Jarrod drummed his fingers on his desk. "Yeah, okay. We'll find a way to make it work."

"Good. I'll keep you posted on how the rest of the trial prep goes." Maddy opened the door and left her boss's office without looking back.

Noah immediately leaped to his feet, his gaze questioning. "Everything okay?"

"Of course. He's more bluster than not." She gave him a rueful smile. "I didn't mention the temporary memory loss. Figured there was no point. But he's up to speed on everything else, including Jackson's murder and our suspicions about Arvani. He's going to use his clout to get a rush on the DNA."

Noah's eyes brightened. "That would be great. I'd like nothing more than to prove the blood belongs to Jackson."

"I know." She brushed past him to reach her desk. His woodsy scent reminded her of their last kiss but she did her best to stay focused on why they were there. To prep her witnesses.

Not to think about how she might find a way to convince him to see her again on a personal level, just the two of them alone, once the trial was over.

"Who's up first?" Noah asked.

His deep voice made her want to smile. "I was supposed to meet with Rachel Graber, Pietro's former girlfriend, but since it's already past ten, it's probably better to focus on Robby Stanford."

"Stanford, Stanford," Noah muttered under his breath. "Why does that name sound familiar?"

She hesitated. "The less you know, the better. Suffice it to say that Robby is currently in jail and is testifying against Pietro in exchange for a reduced sentence."

"Figures," Noah said in a glum voice. "As fast as we get these guys arrested, someone is letting them out on the street again."

Maddy felt her cheeks flush, but bit back a retort. She couldn't deny he was partially right. It wasn't like she enjoyed that part of her job, making deals with low-level criminals to turn against the guys who happened to be higher up in the criminal food chain. But it wasn't as if there was always a better option.

Getting the higher crime bosses off the streets had to be more important. Otherwise it really was all for nothing.

She picked up her phone to call the assistant she shared with the other ADAs. Jarrod Fine was the only one who had his own dedicated assistant.

"Jennifer? I need you to make arrangements for Robby

Stanford to be brought to my office at 12:30. I'll call Rachel Graber to schedule her prep for either later this afternoon or first thing in the morning."

"Will do." Thankfully, Jennifer was cool under pressure; nothing seemed to ruffle the woman's feathers.

"Rachel Graber?" Noah raised an eyebrow. "I'm surprised she's willing to testify against her former boyfriend."

Maddy grimaced. "It hasn't been easy. She's definitely skittish about the whole thing." She thought about the last time she'd seen the young woman, barely legal at twenty-two with eyes that were far older than her years. "Rachel is scared to death of Pietro and so far, our offer of protection is the only thing we have working in our favor."

Noah didn't say anything more as she made the call to Rachel's cell number. She frowned as the call went immediately to voice mail.

"Rachel, it's Maddy. Please call me as soon as possible." She rattled off her office number and then added Noah's disposable cell phone number as an afterthought.

"That's strange," she said. "Rachel normally answers right away."

Noah straightened and leaned forward. "Where is she being held? You need to call her protection detail to make sure everything is okay."

She opened a file on her desk and ran her finger down the list of information, seeking the number of the motel, trying to ignore the ripple of unease. "I'm sure they would have called me if there was a problem."

Noah didn't say anything, waiting until she'd found the number of the detective in charge of the case. She dialed Detective Lowenbaum's number, glancing down at the name of the place she knew Rachel was being held, Greenland Motel.

The detective's phone rang several times, then went to voice mail. She left a message, requesting a call back, then quickly dialed the motel number.

"Greenland Motel, may I help you?"

Finally a person! "Yes, this is ADA Madison Callahan, I'm calling to check on the status of Renee Greer in room 104," she said, using the alias they'd given Rachel.

"Greer. Greer…" The woman's voice trailed off. There was a long silence before she returned to the line. "Would you like me to connect you to the room?"

Relief had her slumping in her seat. "Yes, please."

"One moment." There was a click and then more ringing. Her body tensed as the ringing continued without an answer. After ten rings, the receptionist picked up the call again. "I'm sorry, your party isn't answering the call. Would you like to leave a message?"

"No, thanks, I'll try again later." Maddy dropped the receiver back in the handset and lifted her gaze to Noah's. "Something's wrong. Rachel should have answered. And if she was in the bathroom or something, the officer stationed in her room should have picked up the phone."

Noah's mouth thinned. "Call my lieutenant. Tell him he needs to send a patrol car to check things out."

She reached out to pick up the phone just as it started to ring. The abrupt sound startled her and she fumbled a bit with the receiver before managing to bring it to her ear. "Callahan," she answered in a curt tone.

"Maddy? This is Detective Keith Lowenbaum. I'm sorry to tell you that Rachel Graber is dead."

"Dead? How? When? What happened?" Maddy tightened her grip on the phone, staring at Noah in horror.

"I'm still trying to piece together what happened, but it looks like some sort of drive-by shooting as they were leaving the motel to come see you. One officer was wounded and is currently being treated at Trinity Medical Center, but unfortunately Rachel was declared dead at the scene."

Dead. One of her key witnesses in the case against Pietro had been murdered in cold blood. First the explosion at her condo, not knowing if her friend and roommate was dead or alive, and now this.

Pietro was getting desperate. She wanted to believe that he'd also be careless enough to make mistakes.

But how many more innocent lives would he take before she could figure out who was lashing out on his behalf?

How long before she found a way to lock Alexander Pietro away for the rest of his life?

THIRTEEN

Noah reached across the desk to take Maddy's hand. This case was spiraling way out of control, yet he didn't know how to rein it back in. He hated feeling so helpless.

"I'll be right there," Maddy said. She hung up the receiver, gave his hand a quick squeeze, then pulled away and rose to her feet. "Let's go. I want to see the scene of the crime for myself."

"Maddy, wait." He leaped up and planted his body between her and the office doorway, blocking her ability to leave. "What if this is nothing more than a trap? Pietro's thugs could be lying in wait for you to do just that, head right over to the crime scene."

Her fingers curled into fists. "One of my primary witnesses is dead! How can I just sit here, moving on with my trial prep, knowing that Pietro had her murdered to prevent her from testifying against him? Don't you understand? She died because of me!"

"Because of Pietro," Noah corrected. He stepped forward and gently clasped her shoulders. "You can't blame yourself for everything that's going wrong with this case."

For a moment, tears welled in her eyes, but then she raised her chin and blinked them back. "Logically I know you're right, but it's not easy to let go of the fact that a young woman has died."

His mind flashed to his sister's pale, still features, her body collapsed in a heap on the bathroom floor, the needle hanging out of her arm. Yeah, he understood that kind of guilt only too well. Was he being a hypocrite? Telling Maddy she wasn't to blame for Rachel's death when he still felt responsible for both Rose's and Gina's deaths?

He gave himself a mental shake. The two situations were different. He'd ignored the signs of his sister's addiction and he'd been the one to abruptly break things off with Gina. He was the common link there, but this wasn't the time to get lost in his past mistakes.

"Please don't go to the crime scene," he pleaded in a low voice. "I know it's hard not to, but think about the fact that you've already lost a day of prep. And you have another session scheduled for this afternoon. Robby Stanford's testimony is just as important for your case, isn't it? Especially now?"

A flash of indecision in her eyes caused him to press his point.

"What kind of evidence do you expect to find that the police won't?" Then it hit him. "You don't trust the police, is that it? Do you think someone on the force leaked her location to Pietro's men?"

She briefly closed her eyes, then shook her head. "I'm not sure what to think. They must have some sort of inside help. For one thing, they've been on our heels since Monday, finding us at every turn. And secondly, how else would Pietro's thugs know to look for her at the safe house at the exact moment they were leaving to see me?"

"Good question." He raked his hand over his sandy blond hair. "Could be that someone accidentally told Arvani her location."

"And what if it wasn't an accidental leak? What if someone on the force is working with Arvani?"

He could feel himself wavering, Maddy's blue eyes sucking him in. Steeling his heart, he looked her straight in the eye. "Even if that was the case, there would be a group of officers and detectives working the scene. Don't forget, one of our own was injured by the drive-by. Trust me, MPD will leave no stone unturned as they seek to find those responsible for the shooting."

Her shoulders slumped in defeat beneath his hands and he couldn't stop himself from drawing her close for a warm hug. She didn't resist, tucking her head into the hollow of his shoulder and allowing him to hold her close.

Maddy felt so right in his arms, and he reveled in the way she rested against him. He was humbled by her trust, her faith in him. He wished she'd confide in him about what had happened to her, but he didn't want to push, either. Regardless, he told himself not to get too attached. Their relationship couldn't go beyond friendship.

Why didn't that knowledge make it easier to let her go?

"Okay, you win. I'll stay here." She moved away, raising her head to smile at him. "It's better for me to keep moving forward on this trial."

He reluctantly let her go, missing her the moment she stepped away. "You could ask Judge Dugan for a continuance," he pointed out.

Before the words left his mouth, she was already shaking her head. "No. For one thing, that's exactly what Pietro's lawyer would like. The last thing I want to do is to give them more time to threaten my family and possibly find a way to eliminate more witnesses. No way. The sooner we get into the courtroom, the better."

Deep down, he agreed with her assessment of their precarious situation. He was glad she wasn't heading out to the crime scene, putting herself in danger. Still, the thought of Maddy standing in the courtroom, facing Pietro, made him break out in a cold sweat. Especially since he couldn't sit at her side, offering his protection.

"Well, then." Maddy cleared her throat and went back to take a seat behind her desk. "How about we get a quick sandwich before the deputies at the jail bring Robby over?"

"Sure." He stayed where he was, crossing his arms over his chest. "But send your assistant down for the food, because I'm not leaving you alone."

She sighed and picked up her phone. He listened as she gave Jennifer their orders. She ended the conversation with "I'll have Officer Sinclair give you the cash for our food."

A smile tugged at the corner of his mouth and he dutifully dug a twenty-dollar bill from his pocket. When Jennifer opened the office door, he handed her the money, then resumed his seat across from Maddy.

"What other witnesses are you planning to prep over the next few days?" he asked.

She tipped her head to the side. "I'm not sure I should give you all their names."

He scowled and straightened in the seat. "I thought we'd agreed that I'd be here as your bodyguard."

"Yes, we did agree on that. But I still have to worry about the integrity of the trial." When he opened his mouth to argue, she lifted a hand to stop him. "I have to review my list anyway, so just leave it alone for now, okay?"

He didn't like being in the dark about critical details but gave her a curt nod. She shuffled through the papers on her desk, reviewing her notes and organizing her thoughts.

The knock at the door indicating their food had arrived was a welcome distraction. He bowed his head to pray. "Dear Lord, bless this food and please continue to keep us safe in Your care. Amen."

"Amen," Maddy echoed. She smiled at him but then turned her attention back to her work, setting down her veggie sandwich on occasion to make notes in the margin.

He finished his meal, realizing he had no idea how it had tasted. When Maddy frowned in concentration, he could see a small furrow in her brow, above the bridge of her nose. The fact that he found that dent adorable made him silently admit just how far gone he was.

It was crazy to even consider seeing Maddy again once the trial was over. Their family backgrounds were so different; hers a well-knit cohesive group whereas his was scattered across the globe with barely any contact between them at all. Hers was full of faith, kindness and love; his was filled with guilt, anger and resentment.

The phone on Maddy's desk rang. She picked it up. "Yes? Oh, thanks, please bring him up."

"Robby Stanford?" he asked when she'd replaced the receiver.

"Yes." She took one last bite of her veggie sandwich and then wrapped up what was left and tucked it in her desk drawer. "He's being brought up now."

"Okay." He glanced around her office, thinking it would be a tight fit for the three of them. Tight, but not impossible. "Where do you want me to sit?"

"Outside my office." Maddy barely glanced at him as she gathered her notes in a pile and pulled out a fresh legal pad.

He blinked, then swallowed a burst of anger, fighting to keep his voice even. "I can't protect you from behind a closed door."

"I'm not in danger. Robby won't be armed." She raised her chin in that familiar stubborn way she had. "So yes, you'll need to sit outside."

He didn't like it, not one bit. But before he could continue arguing with her, there was a light rap on the door. He opened it up to see two deputies escorting a skinny kid dressed in prison orange, his wrists cuffed and his ankles chained together. Robby Stanford looked young, barely legal voting age, but there was an aura about him that bespoke of hard living.

"Thanks," Maddy said, bestowing a wide smile on the two deputies. "Appreciate your help. Robby, please take a seat."

Noah didn't like the kid, maybe because he was vying for a reduced sentence for crimes that he should pay for. Considering the cuffs and chains, Noah was forced to admit that the kid was well confined and not likely to be much of a threat. Regardless, leaving the office and closing the door behind him was the hardest thing he'd ever done.

The deputies left and he pulled an uncomfortable-looking hardback chair over to Maddy's closed office door. As he sat down, he could hear the muffled voices inside. Not the specific words but the different cadence to their voices, Maddy's soft melodic voice a stark comparison to Robby's rough, sullen baritone.

Noah let out a heavy sigh and attempted to mentally prepare himself for a long, tedious day. Not easy considering what he really wanted to do was to continue investigating Arvani's potential link to Pietro.

Eliminating the threat to Maddy once and for all.

Maddy took her time with Robby, asking him to repeat what he'd told her during their first meeting. Hopefully his testimony would remain consistent. Certainly something had to go her way in this case, right?

Wrong.

"I don't remember," Robby muttered when she asked him when he first met Alexander Pietro.

Her stomach twisted painfully, and she leveled him with her best no-nonsense glare. "Sure you do. You told me before in great detail how you first met."

Robby avoided her gaze, his shifty eyes moving from his cuffed wrists to the items on her desk to the colorful fall trees in the painting she had hanging on her wall. "Then why are you askin'?"

She strove for patience. "Tell me about the first time you met Alexander Pietro," she repeated.

Robby curled his shoulders in, as if attempting to make himself look smaller. "I told you, I don't remember."

"Fine. Then there's no point in wasting my time." Maddy picked up her phone and pressed the intercom button to reach Jennifer. "I need you to call the two deputies. Stanford is ready to return to his cell."

"Wait!" Robby leaned forward, his expression panicked. "Just wait, okay? I'll tell you!"

"Hang on for a minute, Jennifer." Maddy put her hand over the speaker. "Last chance, Robby. You either take this seriously or I'll send you back to your cell and your deal for a lighter sentence is off the table. Your choice. I'm finished messing around."

"Fine, yeah, okay. I get it." Robby shifted in his seat. "Relax, will ya? Can't you take a joke?"

"No." Maddy removed her hand. "Never mind, Jennifer, don't call the deputies just yet. I'll let you know when we're finished."

"Sounds good," Jennifer agreed.

Maddy replaced the handset in the cradle, battling a wave of exhaustion. The nagging headache had returned, too, but she did her best to ignore it.

Her witness list was getting smaller, so she couldn't afford to lose Robby's testimony. But she'd learned over the past few years to always keep the upper hand, especially when it came to those criminals who were testifying in exchange for a lighter sentence.

"One more time. When did you first meet Alexander Pietro?"

"We'd just gotten our biggest shipment of high-grade junk delivered to the warehouse when he suddenly showed up, demanding to see it for himself." Robby's lips curled in a sneer. "It was like he didn't trust us or something. I knew Alex was the big boss, but I didn't expect him to show up that day out of the blue."

Finally a statement consistent with what he'd originally told her. "Where was the warehouse?"

"On the south side of Milwaukee. The building is about half a block down from the intersection of Birch Street and Carson."

"And what name was on the warehouse?"

"Carson Electronics." Robby smirked. "We kept guns in there, too, along with the drugs."

"What happened next?" she asked, barely looking at her notes. She knew this part of the trial well enough to recite it herself by memory.

She paused for a moment, silently thanking God once again for restoring her memory.

"Well?" she prodded, when Robby didn't answer.

"He made us count out every bag of heroin, making sure each gram was accounted for. Once that was done, he looked us over as if he suspected someone of cheating him."

She raised an eyebrow. "That's different from what you told me last time, Robby. You claimed you didn't have time to count the entire shipment."

Robby averted his gaze once again, lifting one skinny shoulder in a helpless shrug. "So what? Maybe we counted the entire shipment or maybe we didn't. What does it matter?"

She jumped to her feet, the sudden movement causing Robby to shrink further into the chair. She turned her back for a moment, struggling to regain her composure.

What if Robby was lying about that night? What if he fell apart on the witness stand? The deal she'd made with him for a lighter sentence would be all for nothing.

And worse, Pietro could walk away from the trial with an innocent verdict rather than being found guilty.

For a moment, she longed for Noah's reassuring presence. Should she break her own rules by asking him to join her? No, that would only hurt her case in the long term.

Masking her expression to one of indifference, she turned to face Robby. "We're done here. I'm calling off our deal," she said in a blunt tone. "You're not a reliable witness."

Robby's expression turned to outrage. "You can't do that. My lawyer says you can't do that!"

"Your lawyer is wrong," Maddy said. "You haven't held up your side of the deal, which makes the entire agreement null and void." At his blank expression, she inwardly sighed. "In other words, since you won't be testifying against Pietro, there is no deal."

Robby glowered at her for a long moment, then shrugged again. "Whatever."

Whatever? She stared at him, wondering what had changed in the week since she'd last met with him. The only explanation she could come up with was that one of Pietro's men must have gotten to him even in jail.

Serving time must look better than whatever they'd threatened him with.

The tightness returned to her belly and for a moment she remembered reading something about Robby's background. What was it again? She leaned over, shuffling through the messy paperwork scattered about her desk.

Robby suddenly lunged to his feet, his cuffed wrists coming up toward her. She saw a flash of silver and let out a screech, jumping backward in order to avoid the blade.

The tip of the letter opener went through her thin blouse, scratching her abdomen. Her office door flew open and she saw Noah grab hold of Robby, yanking him away from her with enough force to make the younger man's head snap backward.

"Are you all right?" Noah asked harshly, leaning heavily on Robby to keep him pinned to the chair. He wrestled the opener away and tossed it far out of the criminal's reach. "Did he hurt you?"

"I—I'm fine," she managed, looking down at the slit the letter opener had made in her blouse. The scratch was barely bleeding, yet the realization of how much worse this could have been made her feel dizzy.

She'd almost been stabbed the same way Matthew had been eighteen months ago.

Worse, this attempt was mostly her fault, for allowing Robby to get his hands on her letter opener. She should have known better than to turn her back on a drug-and-gun dealer.

"What happened?" Noah asked. "How did he get the weapon?"

"My fault. I never should have had it on my desk." She looked at Robby, seeing the frank fear in his eyes for the first time. "Why did you do it, Robby?"

The eighteen-year-old's hazel eyes filled with tears. "Pietro threatened to kill my mother. He told me to kill you." Tears rolled down his cheeks, making him look twelve. "I had to do it, don't you see? He'll kill my mother! She's taking care of my younger brother and sister. What will happen to them if she dies? I had to do it, I had to!"

Maddy closed her eyes and pressed her fingertips against her forehead. The anguish in Robby's tone was all too real. And she could identify with his fear.

After all, hadn't Pietro's goon said the same thing to her? *Drop the case or everyone you care about will die, including the two old ladies living in the house on the hill.*

Jennifer's voice through the intercom interrupted her thoughts. "I've called the deputies. They're coming back ASAP."

Maddy dropped her hand from her head and nodded. "Thanks, Jennifer." She knew her assistant had noticed Noah leaping into the office to save her life.

Again.

"Robby Stanford, you're under arrest for assault with a deadly weapon," Noah said. "You have the right to remain silent, anything you say can and will be used against you in a court of law…"

"Stop it, Noah," she interrupted. "I'm not pressing charges."

"What?" Noah drilled her with a furious glare. "Why not? He tried to kill you, Maddy."

"Because he's afraid of Pietro. Because someone got to him even while he was in jail." She shifted her gaze to Robby and tried to hide her trembling hands from Noah's eagle gaze. "Didn't they?"

The tears continued rolling down his cheeks. "Y-yes."

She sighed, struggling to remain calm. She was losing her witnesses faster than a dried-out Christmas tree lost its pine needles.

And she had no idea how to stop the destruction surrounding her case.

FOURTEEN

"I still think you should press charges." Noah's heart thundered in his chest, the impact of Maddy's close call hitting him hard. So close. If she hadn't jumped back in time, if he hadn't busted through her door when he had... He swallowed hard.

Unbelievable that she was nearly stabbed, just like Matthew. There was actually a small tear in her blouse from the letter-opener blade.

Robby squirmed beneath his heavy grasp. He could tell that Maddy was buying Robby's story about his mother being threatened by Pietro's men, so Noah forced himself to relax his hold on the kid's shoulders. But he didn't let go.

Maddy sighed, her expression full of regret. "Robby, will you testify against Pietro if we send your mother and siblings away from here to keep them safe?"

"I think he should testify in exchange for you not pressing charges against him for assault with a deadly weapon," Noah said, his tone harsh. "Just because he's scared doesn't mean he can try to kill you."

Unfortunately she ignored him, her attention riveted on Robby Stanford. "Well?" she pressed. "Will you do it?"

Robby swiped his face against the orange jumpsuit cov-

ering his upper arm. "What about me?" he asked. "If I testify, Pietro will kill me, too."

"After the trial, we'll move you to a facility out of state,"
Maddy said. "You'll remain in isolation, without contact
with the other prisoners until then." When Robby started
to shake his head—no one liked being left alone, even for
their own protection—Maddy's voice hardened. "That's
the best I can do, Robby. The trial starts on Monday, and
I'll move you up on the schedule so that you're not in the
jail here for very long."

Robby's expression was indecisive.

"You better take her offer," Noah warned. "The fact
that you failed to take Maddy out means your mother is
still in danger. How will you feel if Pietro seeks revenge
on her for your failure?"

The logic of Noah's statement must have gotten through
to Robby because the kid finally nodded in agreement. As
if on cue, the two deputies from the jail arrived.

"What happened?" the deputy named Olson asked.

"Nothing happened. False alarm," Maddy said with a
weary smile. "Although I think we're finished for the day.
Please instruct the warden to keep my witness protected
and isolated from the other prisoners until he testifies. I
don't want anything untoward to happen to him before
the trial."

The deputies exchanged a questioning glance, then
Olson shrugged. "Sure. Anything else?"

"I may need to work with Mr. Stanford again tomorrow. I'll let you know what time."

"Okay," Deputy Olson said. He and his partner each
grabbed one of Robby Stanford's arms and hauled him to
his feet. The kid didn't resist and for a brief moment, the
resigned expression in the boy's eyes gave Noah a sense

of hope that the kid would actually follow through with his promise to testify against Pietro.

Thanks to Maddy.

Watching her in action was something. Noah couldn't deny that Maddy had been able to turn a potentially catastrophic situation into something that worked out in her favor. And he didn't doubt for one moment that she'd attempt to make good on her part of their bargain.

Although, ensuring Robby's and his family's safety from the long reach of Pietro wouldn't be easy, but he knew she'd do everything possible to make that happen.

If only he could be as certain of her safety. First Pietro's girlfriend, Rachel, then this.

What next? He wished he knew.

Noah and Maddy remained silent until Robby and the deputies had disappeared from the office suite. He regarded her warily, trying to gauge her mood. "Are you ready to call it quits for the day?" he asked.

She grimaced. "I shouldn't. There's still so much to do. And it's bothering me that we haven't heard anything from Gretchen, either."

He hated to admit that the lack of news related to her roommate didn't bode well. "We need to head back to the safety of our motel. Gather up what you'll need to keep working from there and I'll check with my boss about what we know so far about the explosion in your building."

She didn't look thrilled with the plan, but didn't argue. While she gathered up her things, he used her desk phone to call Lieutenant O'Grady, placing the call on speaker.

"What?" O'Grady snarled in lieu of a greeting.

"This is Sinclair," Noah identified himself. "I'm looking for an update on the explosion at ADA Callahan's condo."

"The smoke eaters have the fire under control," his boss said. "That's as much as I know."

"Has there been any mention of casualties?" Noah pressed. "They must have some idea by now if anyone was near the blast."

"Hey, you want answers? Call the ADA's brother. Mitch Callahan is the arson specialist assigned to investigate the fire."

"Thanks." Noah disconnected and looked at Maddy. "Do you know Mitch's number off the top of your head?"

"Yes. Here, I'll dial." She punched in the numbers and then hit the speaker button on her phone so they could both talk.

"Callahan."

"Mitch? It's Maddy. I need to know if anyone has gotten in touch with Gretchen."

"Maddy, I'm so glad you're all right." The relief in Mitch's tone was evident. "So far we haven't identified any casualties from the blast, although the source appears to be on the third floor, near the elevator."

Her gaze clashed with Noah's. Noah remembered the door to her condo wasn't far from the elevator. "I haven't heard from Gretchen and I'm worried about her," Maddy confessed. "I'm fairly certain that bomb was meant for me."

"Yeah, that's the primary theory at the moment," Mitch said in a flat tone. "I assume this is related to your upcoming trial, same as the threat against Mom and Nan?"

"I'm afraid so." Maddy's expression was full of contrition, a fact that made Noah angry. Maddy and her family shouldn't have to live in fear just because she was doing her job.

"It's not Maddy's fault," Noah spoke up defensively. "Pietro is getting desperate. Once the trial is over, things will get back to normal."

"Who's that with you?" Mitch demanded.

"Noah Sinclair," Maddy answered. "He's my self-proclaimed bodyguard."

"Hrmph." Mitch didn't seem impressed. There were voices in the background, then Mitch said, "Listen, I have to go. I'll let you know if I find out anything about Gretchen, okay?"

"Thanks, Mitch, take care." Maddy hung up. "I'm going to call Gretchen's cell phone one more time."

Noah nodded, understanding her concern. As the phone rang and rang, she finished shoving her paperwork into a large accordion file. She left her roommate another message, her expression grim. "Let's go."

He nodded, more than ready to return to the relative anonymity of the motel. He guarded Maddy closely, keeping himself between her and any potential threat as they made their way back down through the back entrance to the parking garage.

Robby's attempt on Maddy replayed itself over and over in his mind as they wove between stationary vehicles, taking a circuitous route to the borrowed truck. Even after he'd helped Maddy inside, Noah couldn't relax, not until they'd reached the street level without incident, leaving the courthouse and her office behind.

Daylight was beginning to fade thanks to the clouds gathering overhead and the upcoming winter solstice. Noah hoped they weren't in for a snowstorm. He and Maddy hadn't had time to listen to the news; for all he knew, a blizzard could be on the way.

Although he couldn't deny the idea of being snowed in with Maddy held a certain appeal. At least as far as keeping her safe.

"I forgot to thank you," Maddy said, breaking into his thoughts. "For rushing to my rescue."

He shrugged. "Not necessary. That's my job."

She wrinkled her nose. "No, it's not. I still can't believe he grabbed my letter opener. It all happened so fast…" Her voice trailed off.

"I know." And he did. Hadn't his split-second hesitation caused her twin brother to be stabbed eighteen months ago?

Her small cold fingers closed over his in an unexpected gesture of comfort. "I'm sorry, Noah. I know I mentioned this before, but Robby's attempt to hurt me made me realize even more just how unfair it was of me to blame you for Matt's injury."

She was being far too kind. "I hesitated that night," he said abruptly. "The second I waited to act was enough for that girl to stab your brother."

"Don't, Noah. Stop taking the blame, all right?" Her tone was testy now. "I understand why Matt told me to forgive you, so you need to do the same."

"Did Matt mention my younger sister, Rose, who died of a heroin overdose?"

She sucked in a harsh breath. "What? No! Oh, Noah, I'm so sorry. What happened?"

He kept one eye on the road, the other watching his rearview mirror to make sure they weren't being followed. "I was in my first year of college and had come home for spring break. Rose was a senior in high school. I knew that she'd been looking bad recently, and I was determined to confront her about it. But I never got the chance. The following morning, I found her lying on the bathroom floor, a needle stuck in her arm. The syringe contained remnants of heroin."

Her fingers tightened on his. "How terrible for you."

For a moment, he glanced at their clasped hands, wishing things could be different. "That girl who stabbed Matt… I saw Rose in her eyes. The desperate need for drugs. That's why I was so determined to bring Pietro to justice. I only wish I'd have confronted Rose much sooner."

"Oh, Noah," Maddy said with a sigh. "Do you know how many times I played the what-if game? What if my dad hadn't gone to the crime scene that day? What if he'd retired the year before when he'd been offered the chance? Don't you see? This is all part of God's plan. We have to put our faith and our trust in Him."

God's plan? Taking Rose at eighteen? Taking Maddy's father? Gina? Those were hard pills to swallow, yet maybe she was right. Maybe each of those events had brought him and Maddy together now.

God was trusting Noah to keep her safe. And that was one mission in which he was determined to succeed.

No matter what.

Maddy wasn't sure if she'd gotten through to Noah or not. She was touched that he'd told her about his past, and she could understand why he was so determined to do whatever was necessary to keep Pietro behind bars. Alexander Pietro wasn't the only source of heroin in the city, but he was one of the largest suppliers. Getting him off the streets had put a nice dent in the illegal drug business.

Thinking about all the adversity Noah had faced, his sister's overdose, then his girlfriend's death in college, humbled her. In retrospect, she'd been extremely fortunate to have her family and her faith to lean on in times of stress and adversity. Her family had come together after her father's murder, supporting one another and keeping on with the family traditions.

Who had helped and supported Noah?

She debated telling him about what had happened with Blake, the secret shame she hadn't shared with anyone else, but then the moment was gone. Noah pulled into the parking lot of the motel, driving around the building to park out of sight from the road.

A few minutes later, they were safe inside their connecting rooms. She set her file folder on the small table next to her computer and wondered where to start.

"Will you allow me to help?" Noah asked, his deep baritone voice causing her to flush with awareness. "Please?"

How could she deny him after what he'd told her about his sister's death? Very simply, she couldn't. There had to be something she could give him that wouldn't compromise her case.

She rifled through her notes and found the description of the warehouse where Noah and his fellow officers had taken down Pietro.

"Will you look at this and see if you can find any other spots where Pietro's men could have a secret stash of either drugs or weapons? The stuff you found that day of his arrest was impressive, but I heard from you and several others that you always suspected there was more than one spot Pietro used."

"Absolutely." Noah took the paperwork from her hand. "It's good for me to review this again, now that we know Arvani is a suspect."

"Great. I'm going to review my trial notes, see if anything else jumps out at me."

"Shall I make a small pot of coffee?" Noah asked.

She smiled. "I'd like that."

The table was cramped with both of them seated there, but she didn't mind. In fact, being here with Noah, working toward the same goal, was nice.

Better than nice. Amazing. She'd never experienced this level of camaraderie before. Not with a man.

Especially not since the incident with Blake.

Enough, she inwardly chided. This wasn't the time to

think about her personal life. She had the biggest trial of her career to prepare for. Witnesses to prep.

Yet all she could think about was Noah's strength. His kindness. His kiss.

"What?" He raised his gaze to meet hers.

She blushed, belatedly realizing she'd been staring at him. "Um, nothing. I was just thinking." *About throwing myself into your arms.*

His smile lit up his entire face. "I like working with you, too."

For a moment, she wondered if she'd spoken her wistful thoughts out loud, but then he went back to reviewing the paperwork in front of him.

She took a deep breath and followed suit. Thankfully, her notes were extensive. She'd been smart enough to complete a lot of work before the night of her attack.

There were still three officers on her list that she hadn't spoken to in several weeks, so she made a note of their names, determined to complete those prep meetings tomorrow. She took her time going through the list of accomplices Noah's team had arrested that night, wondering if she could lean on any of them to turn on Pietro. According to her notes, they'd all refused to talk, but that had been almost three weeks ago.

Maybe now they'd reconsider. Although truly, it wasn't likely. Still, she needed to ask, so she began to make a list of everyone she needed to talk to before Monday.

There were a lot of things to do before Monday. What if she couldn't get them all completed? A wave of helplessness hit, but she shoved it back.

Failure was not an option.

"Maddy?" Noah's voice was a welcome distraction.

"Did you find something?" She leaned forward, eager for good news.

"I think so." His tone was thoughtful. He tugged his chair closer and showed her the map of the city he'd brought up on her computer. "There are two buildings, one here and here." He pointed to the spots on the screen. "They're both owned by Chicago businessmen."

"Chicago." Her eyes widened. "You think they may be linked to Arvani?"

"It's possible. They're both within ten miles of the arrest site." He shrugged good-naturedly. "Or it could be nothing."

"You don't really believe that, or you wouldn't have pointed them out." She stared at the places he'd identified. "Those are both located in sketchy parts of the city. I'm not sure we should head over yet tonight, maybe it's better to wait until morning?"

Before Noah had a chance to answer, his disposable phone rang. He lifted it to his ear. "Sinclair."

Maddy watched his face, trying to gauge his reaction.

"Gretchen? Okay, hang on, she's right here." He handed her the phone. "It's for you."

Maddy took the phone, her heart in her throat. "Gretchen? Are you okay?"

"Maddy? What's going on? What happened to our building?" Her roommate's voice was full of fear.

"I'm so glad you're safe!" Tears of relief welled in her eyes. "I've been so worried about you. I'm glad you weren't in the condo when the bomb went off."

"Me, too," Gretchen agreed. "Your brother Mitch is here. He's claiming you were the intended victim. Is that true? Was the explosion meant for you?"

"It's likely, but hasn't been proved yet one way or the other."

"I can't believe it," Gretchen murmured. "What if you and I had been home? We would have been killed!"

Maddy had a bad feeling her friend was about to lose it. "I'm sorry, Gretchen. I know this is difficult, but the trial will be over soon and everything will return to normal."

"Oh, yeah? You mean until your next trial, don't you?" Her roommate's tone was bitter. "No, thanks, Maddy. If you don't mind, I think I'll look for a new place to live. Your condo is beyond destroyed now anyway."

"Gretchen, wait…" *Click.* Maddy pulled the phone from her ear, staring at the blank screen.

"That didn't sound good," Noah said, taking the phone from her fingers. "I'm sorry."

"Me, too." Maddy couldn't blame Gretchen for wanting to distance herself from the criminals Maddy worked to put behind bars.

Losing Gretchen's friendship was just one more casualty in her battle against Pietro. She dropped her head in her hand, trying to hold it together.

"Come here." Noah pulled her upright and into his arms, holding her close. "It's okay. Give her some time. She might come around."

"I don't think so," she whispered.

Noah stroked his hand over her hair, pressing her cheek against his chest. "I'm sorry, Maddy. You've been through a lot over these past few days."

"Yes, and so have you." She wanted so badly to kiss him, but the last time she'd done that he'd pulled away. If he rejected her again, she wasn't sure how she'd handle it.

If only she could find a way to show him how much she liked being with him. Not just working together, but being close to him.

Noah must have read her mind, because he pressed his mouth against her temple in a soft kiss. Then he moved to her cheek, the sweetness of his kiss making her heart race.

She waited, practically holding her breath until he

placed his finger beneath her chin, tipping her face up so he could cover her mouth with his.

Clinging to his shoulders, she lost herself in his kiss. Noah's embrace felt like coming home.

FIFTEEN

Noah knew he should have resisted the temptation to kiss her, but she'd looked so lost, so forlorn, he hadn't been able to help himself.

And now that he'd tasted her sweetness again, he didn't want to stop.

In some tiny corner of his mind, he reveled in the fact that beautiful, smart Maddy Callahan was holding on to him, kissing him back. He had no idea what he'd done to deserve such a precious gift, and he didn't want to let her go.

But the need to breathe eventually had him raising his head, burying his face against her hair, inhaling her cinnamon scent. His heart pounded erratically in his chest and it took a significant amount of effort to gather his scattered brain cells together long enough to form a coherent thought.

He wondered again what had happened to her in the past, who had tried to hurt her, but before he could ask, his phone rang. The loudness had the same effect as having a bucket of ice water dumped on his head.

"It may be related to the case," Maddy said.

"I know." He didn't completely let her go, but reached

into his pocket to pull out his phone. "Sinclair," he said, his voice rougher than normal.

"We have ballistics back on the slugs recovered at the Racine Marina," O'Grady said bluntly. "They came from a Smith & Wesson M&P 15 tactical rifle."

Instantly Noah's brain cleared. "The same weapon the Milwaukee police department transitioned to last year."

"Yeah," his boss agreed. "Anyone can buy one, but it's interesting that it's a known cop weapon. And many police departments have been using them."

Like Chicago? Noah intended to find out. "What about the blood sample I gave you? What's taking so long to get a simple blood type?"

Lieutenant O'Grady grunted. "I'll see what I can do. Any new information from your end?"

Noah quickly filled him in on the drive-by shooting death of Maddy's witness Rachel Graber. "She was Pietro's girlfriend," he finished. "If we keep losing witnesses, there won't be a trial."

"I need your expertise in following up on all these loose ends," his boss said. "Can't Callahan's brothers keep an eye on her?"

"She's still in danger. One of her witnesses, Robby Stanford, attempted to stab her earlier today. There have been threats against her family, too, so two of her brothers, Matthew and Mike, are taking turns staying at her mother's house. Mitch is investigating the fire at her condo."

"Miles and Marc are keeping an eye on their own families," she added in a soft voice. "It wouldn't be fair to put the children at risk." Maddy gently pushed away from him. He reluctantly let her go.

He gave those details to O'Grady. "Look, I'd like your permission to stay close to Maddy for now. I'll check in as often as I can, okay?"

"Fine." His boss wasn't happy, but stopped arguing. "See that you do."

Maddy frowned. "I don't like interfering with your ability to do your job," she said when he hung up the phone. "I can talk to my brothers, maybe there's a way to make it all work out."

"No," Noah said with more force than he intended, every cell in his body rejecting that idea. "I'm not leaving you, Maddy. Besides, it won't be much longer, the trial is just a few days away."

"As of tomorrow morning it will be four days away, that's longer than a few," she countered, but her tone lacked conviction. She stayed close and he couldn't deny liking the fact that she liked being with him.

Was he crazy to think there was something more than friendship growing between them? The kisses they'd shared couldn't be ignored. But what if her feelings toward him changed once the danger was over?

Wait a minute. Maybe Maddy had come to depend on him for protection, but he was still the same man who'd let down his sister and his former girlfriend.

Besides, if things didn't work out between him and Maddy, her brothers would come after him and rightly so. Hurting her would be far worse than hurting himself.

He took a slight step backward, forcing himself to think about the case. What had he been working on? Oh, yeah, the two warehouses owned by people who lived in Chicago.

"I think we should take a drive past those two warehouses," he said.

Maddy wrinkled her nose. "It's dark and both of them happen to be in a rough part of town. We should wait until morning."

He didn't want to wait until morning, but driving by

once wasn't really going to help. He suddenly snapped his fingers. "Cameras," he said. "That's what we need, small trail cameras pointed at the warehouse entrances. That way we can run video and see who's going in and out."

She hesitated. "We wouldn't be able to use a secret surveillance video in court."

"We could if the camera is posted on public property," he argued. "There is no expectation of privacy on a public street."

"That's true," she agreed, although her expression held skepticism. "If we can find some public property to use. Other buildings in the area or across the street are likely private property."

He wasn't about to give up the idea. "There's bound to be a lamppost or telephone pole nearby. But we need to buy the cameras before the stores close. Ready?"

She glanced down at her notes for a moment, then shrugged. "Why not?"

It didn't take them long to drag on their winter coats to head back outside. The snow was falling now in soft gentle flakes, pretty yet covering the road enough to cause hazardous driving conditions.

Remembering how his squad car had been rammed into Lake Michigan made him grateful that Matt had provided them with a four-wheel-drive truck. Not that he had any intention of getting too close to the lakeshore.

The sporting-goods store was busy with Christmas shoppers. He and Maddy blended in, edging through the crowd to find the trail cameras. They were pricey, especially the ones with motion sensors that turned on the video streaming when there was activity nearby.

Reading a box, he frowned when he realized that there were only thirty-six hours of video available. Good for hunters in the woods, but not so good when using them in the city when there would be a lot more people and traffic. But it was better than nothing, so he purchased four devices, hoping to install two of them at each warehouse. They needed to be mounted, so he added black electrical tape and zip ties, as well.

He didn't want to drag Maddy along with him to get these installed, yet he didn't want to leave her alone, either. He inwardly debated the pros and cons as they stood in a long line of customers for almost twenty minutes. Finally he paid the bill and carried the supplies out to the truck.

"I guess we should wait until later to install these, right?" Maddy asked once they were back on the road.

"Yeah, that's what I was thinking." He didn't add the part where once Maddy fell asleep, he'd call her brother to come stay at the motel for a bit while he mounted the cameras.

She swiveled toward him. "Don't even think of going without me."

How had she known what he was thinking? Was his face really that transparent?

"I know how you think," Maddy went on as if he'd spoken out loud. "But it's best if there are two of us—one to do the work and one to keep watch."

Since she had a point, he grudgingly nodded. "Okay. In the meantime, let's get something to eat."

"I could eat. However, we should also find these warehouses, see what we're up against. We may need additional supplies."

He'd tried to plan ahead with the zip ties and electrical tape, but she was right. They might need something more. The first warehouse was located south of the area where they'd taken down Pietro, so he drove there first.

Houses grew more and more dilapidated until they disappeared altogether, leaving nothing but old structures, many with broken windows and bars across the doors. The warehouse he was looking for, owned by George Lamb from Chicago, was the last building on a dead-end street.

Noah felt a bit as if their truck had a bull's-eye painted on it as he quickly turned around. Maddy kept her gaze focused on her passenger-side window, looking for anything out of place. And for spots where they could legally mount their cameras.

"I saw an old, abandoned telephone pole," Maddy said once they'd left the area. "But the fact that it's on a dead end adds a new element. We'll have to park a few blocks away and go in on foot."

"I'll manage, not a problem," he assured her. "Let's check out the other site."

Maddy nodded, settling back in her seat. The second location was owned by Moving and Storage, Inc. No name was listed, just a Chicago address.

Moving and Storage, Inc. happened to be in even a worse part of the area. As Noah turned onto 3rd Street, a large truck was backing away from the warehouse in question.

"Get down, but help me get the license plate number," he said, making a quick turn into the driveway of a two-story home that looked as if a strong wind could blow it over. Dousing the lights and turning off the engine, he slid down in the seat, hoping the driver of the truck wouldn't notice them sitting there.

Maddy slouched down, too, her eyes wide in the darkness. When the truck lumbered past, she quickly turned and stared at the license plate.

"55-TFRU," she said. "Although the F could be an E. I can't say for sure."

He repeated the number and letter sequence until he had it memorized, then quickly dialed the MPD dispatch in his district. "This is Officer Sinclair. I need the name registered to 55-TFRU."

The clacking of keys could be heard in the background, then the dispatcher said, "Peter Durango is listed as the owner."

The name meant nothing. Maddy touched his arm. "Try 55-TERU."

He repeated his request with the new license plate number and this time the dispatcher responded quicker. "Owner is listed as a corporation, Moving and Storage, Inc."

"Thanks." Noah hung up and turned to Maddy. "We need your computer. I want to know who exactly owns the company."

"Let's grab a pizza on the way back," Maddy agreed.

He liked the way she thought, and restarted the truck. "First I need to see the layout around the warehouse." He twisted the key, bringing the engine to life, then slowly backed out of the driveway. A light pole was located a good block away from the building, yet well within line of sight of the warehouse.

Perfect.

Satisfied they had a good plan, he drove around the block, then headed for the interstate. They picked up a pizza from a place not far from their motel, half veggie for her, the works for him.

Inside, he set the pizza down, then went straight to the computer. He searched again for the owner of Moving and Storage, Inc., digging deeper this time, wishing he'd done that before getting the cameras.

The enticing aroma of pizza caused his stomach to growl, nearly derailing him from his mission. Then he found it, the name on the screen hitting him hard.

"What is it?" Maddy asked, coming to lean over his

shoulder. She sucked in a harsh breath and he nodded, knowing this was exactly the link they needed.

"Lance Arvani." He turned to look up at her. "Do you think this is enough to get a search warrant?"

She grimaced. "Not yet. What do we have other than seeing your partner's truck outside his cabin?"

He knew she was right. He didn't like it, but the law was there to protect the rights of the innocent.

"Once we get the blood test results back, we may have enough for a warrant," she added.

Noah nodded. The results should be back by tomorrow. One more day couldn't hurt. Especially since he still planned on mounting the cameras.

He'd find the proof he needed to put Arvani and anyone else working for Pietro away for good.

Maddy dropped into the seat beside Noah, her thoughts tumbling around in her brain. Should she try to get a search warrant? There wasn't any hard evidence, but maybe it was worth a shot.

Then again, disturbing a judge this late in the evening would likely get her head bitten off. No, they needed something more. The truck belonging to a dead cop wasn't enough.

Noah surprised her by clasping her hand in his and bowing his head. "Dear Lord, we thank You for this food we are about to eat and we ask for Your help in keeping us safe in Your care. Amen."

She smiled and gently squeezed his hand. "Amen."

"Dig in," Noah said lightly. For a moment she flashed back to when her father was alive, sitting at the head of the table. It bothered her that the police had never been able to find the person who'd shot him. Or even a true motive as to why he'd been murdered. She knew both Miles and Matt had tried to get answers, but to no avail. She'd dug a bit into the mystery, too, going through some of the court cases in which her father had played a role in the indictment.

But she hadn't found anything yet. Mostly because her real job had taken over her life, especially this particular case. But maybe once the Pietro trial was over, she could go back to spending her free time digging into her father's case. Especially since she didn't have much of a personal life.

She glanced at Noah beneath her lashes, remembering every second of their last kiss. She liked Noah, more than she should.

He was the first man in months whose touch hadn't made her jerk away in fear. Odd how her amnesia had actually helped her get over that fear of men. Since that night, she'd been with Noah nonstop.

Her cheeks heated as she recalled just how much she'd enjoyed Noah's touch. His kiss. Being held in his arms.

Stop it! This wasn't the time to be thinking about romance. She was being terrorized by a murderer who was not just threatening her family but trying to systematically kill off her key witnesses.

Focus, she told herself. They had important things to do. Kissing Noah again wasn't one of them.

"Maddy? Are you all right?"

She snapped her head up, meeting his concerned gaze. He was already on his second slice of pizza, whereas she hadn't touched her first. "Yes, of course." She lifted a slice and took a healthy bite. "It's great."

"I think we should mount the cameras at the warehouse owned by Moving and Storage, Inc., first. That's our more likely target."

"Agreed. Although we shouldn't ignore the other warehouse, either. We might get something from that one, as well." The idea of shutting down more of the heroin and gun trade gave her a sense of satisfaction.

"I think we should wait until about midnight, then head out," Noah said thoughtfully.

That seemed a bit too early, but she was afraid that if she went to bed to get some sleep, Noah might sneak out to go alone. Unacceptable. She wanted to be there, at least as a lookout and helper.

"Fine with me," she said, finishing one slice and reaching for another. "Can you think of any other supplies we may need?"

He shook his head. "No, besides, it's too late to pick up anything else. The cameras don't have to be mounted super high, just enough to record the activity at the doorway."

They finished the rest of their meal in silence. When she finished, she began cleaning up the mess. Noah pulled out the spare bulletproof vest and handed it to her. "Put this on just in case, okay?"

"Sure." She took the vest along with the sweatshirt Noah had purchased for her and disappeared into the bathroom to change. The vest was as bulky as she remembered, but there was no point in complaining. She knew Noah was wearing his, as well.

Hopefully, they wouldn't need them.

Noah went through the equipment, checking each device to be sure they were working. Then he replaced everything in the bag and opened the door for her.

Once again they walked back out in the cold December night. The snow flurries had stopped, but the clouds overhead still obscured any light from the moon.

A strange sense of foreboding hit hard as Noah drove toward the warehouse. She told herself the darkness was their friend; it would help hide them and the cameras.

So why the strange sense of dread?

The trip down to the warehouse didn't take long. They arrived twenty minutes before their designated midnight time frame. Noah parked a block away, then turned in his seat. "Do you have your disposable phone?"

She nodded, pulling it out of her pocket. It rang in her hand, startling her. She pressed the talk button and immediately realized the caller was Noah.

"Let's keep the connection open—that way if either of us needs something, all we have to do is to say so. Okay?"

"I like it," she agreed. Knowing she could hear Noah if something bad happened made her feel better.

He leaned forward and gave her a quick, unexpected kiss before sliding out from behind the wheel. He closed the driver-side door behind him with a loud click.

She sat for a minute, a bemused expression on her face. Once Pietro was permanently behind bars, she was absolutely going to find a way to convince Noah to give them a chance.

He was wrong about not doing relationships. She suspected he'd do just fine with the right woman.

With her.

A muffled grunt reached her ears, drawing her attention to the issue at hand. She heard more sounds of movement, then Noah's voice suddenly spoke in her ear. "Maddy?"

"What's wrong?"

"There's a guy walking toward the warehouse," he said, speaking in a low whisper. "I think I'm going crazy, because the guy looks an awful lot like Jackson."

She frowned, thinking she must have heard wrong. "Your partner? That can't be right. We watched him die!"

"I know, but I'm telling you, it's either Jackson or his identical twin. Either way, I'm following him."

Maddy straightened in her seat, fumbling with her seat belt. "Noah, wait!"

But he didn't respond and in her heart, she knew he wasn't about to stop.

Filled with a steely determination, she pushed open her door and jumped down to the ground. If Noah was going into the warehouse, then so was she.

They were in this together.

SIXTEEN

The man making his way down the street toward the warehouse wore a heavy winter coat and a black knit hat, but there was just enough bright red hair peeking out beneath the fabric to draw Noah's attention.

He was short, rather stocky and had red hair. Just like his partner Jackson Dellis. But that wasn't possible. Jackson was dead.

Wasn't he?

Yes. He and Maddy had watched him get shot in the chest, watched him crumple to the ground in a heap. So this guy couldn't be Jackson. Unless his partner had a brother? Someone who looked just like him?

The fact that the man was walking up toward the warehouse they'd already linked to Lance Arvani was enough to escalate Noah's suspicions to frank alarm. Was Jackson's brother working for Arvani? Had his partner been shot by his own flesh and blood?

Noah didn't know, but he intended to find out.

He finished mounting the camera, making sure it was pointed toward the doorway across the street. He spoke softly as he moved away so that Maddy could hear him through his phone. If she knew what was going on, maybe she wouldn't worry.

The alarm in her tone when he'd left the truck bothered him, but not enough to make him hesitate. He pulled his weapon and darted across the street. He sidled up to the side of the warehouse, staying in the shadows, then peeked around the corner.

The guy who looked like Jackson's double glanced over his shoulder, as if sensing Noah's gaze, then went up to the side door next to the loading dock. He opened the door without using a key and walked inside.

Well, that was interesting. There didn't seem to be anyone positioned outside the door to stand guard, so maybe the warehouse didn't contain drugs or guns. Usually valuable items like that warranted some sort of patrol.

Then again, the armed guards could be stationed inside.

A sudden movement off to the left had Noah bracing himself for a possible attack. He turned to glance over and nearly choked when he saw Maddy heading toward him. He scowled and tried to wave her back, but she ignored him. She was talking on her phone, although he didn't know who she was talking to, since their call had ended. She appeared to finish up the conversation, tucking the device back into her pocket. She lightly jogged toward him, her expression full of determination.

Noah didn't like it, but hung back waiting for her to catch up to him. He grasped her arm and drew her close to the building so they were both out of sight.

"What are you doing here?" he asked in a harsh whisper.

She glared at him. "Did you really think I was going to sit in the truck doing nothing? I called for backup. Matt is on his way."

Having backup wasn't a bad thing, especially his former partner who he missed working with more than he'd thought possible. But at the same time, he didn't want Maddy anywhere near the danger. "Good job calling Matt for help. But I need you to wait out here, okay? You're not armed."

Her frown deepened. "Oh, yeah? Well, I don't want you going in alone, either. Let's wait for Matt. Are you sure that the guy you saw was Jackson?"

"No, I'm not sure of anything right now. He sure looked like Jackson Dellis, but I only caught a glimpse of his face in the dark. Dellis never mentioned having a brother, but it's possible that's who I saw heading inside. I'd really like to check for myself to be sure."

"Do we have probable cause?" Maddy asked.

He raised his brow. "A man who was shot in front of our eyes went inside the building owned by the man we suspected of shooting him. I think that's enough for probable cause." At least, he hoped so.

She didn't look convinced. "So what's the crime in progress?"

There were times when being teamed up with a lawyer wasn't much fun. Like now. He thought fast. "Aiding and abetting a murderer."

Maddy rolled her eyes and shook her head. "We need to come up with something better than that."

He hunched his shoulders against the wind and glanced around the area along the side of the warehouse. He firmly believed there were illegal activities going on inside, headed up by none other than Chicago police officer Lance Arvani, but Maddy was correct in that the law required proof. Then again, claiming to see his dead partner would only make him look crazy, rather than working in his favor. If the front door was open and not locked, he wouldn't be forced to break in. One minor point in his favor.

If only they had something more. He looked around; at first he saw a whole lot of nothing. Then a sliver of brass caught his eye. Noah moved forward and squatted on his haunches, peering down at the ground.

"What is it?" Maddy whispered.

He carefully picked up the bullet with his gloved fingers, attempting to preserve any potential prints, and showed it to Maddy. "This is the same ammo that's used in the Smith & Wesson M&P 15 tactical rifle. Matches the slugs found at the crime scene at the Racine Marina." He rose to his feet. "I think that's enough of a link to establish probable cause, don't you?"

She reluctantly nodded. "Yeah, that works."

His phone vibrated and he pulled out the device. His boss. Stifling a sigh, he answered. "Sinclair."

"We have some interesting results on the blood you found on the ground in Arvani's driveway," O'Grady said bluntly.

Noah's pulse spiked with anticipation. "Yeah? What?"

"It's not human. Belongs to the bovine family."

His gaze crashed with Maddy's as he grappled with the news. "Cow's blood? I don't understand."

"Me, either. Can you explain how else the blood got there? You thought it belonged to your partner, but that's obviously not the case."

O'Grady was right about that. He and Maddy had been there when the shot was fired. They had watched Jackson go down. But what if that was nothing but a big show?

He sagged against the side of the building. Why would Jackson do something like that? Noah didn't understand what his partner and his accomplice had hoped to gain from the charade.

Other than maybe setting a trap to kill him and Maddy?

And if that didn't work, framing Noah for his murder?

The more he considered that option, the more it grew on him. Especially since he'd almost rushed forward with

Maddy to meet Jackson when he'd stepped out of his truck at the marina. Only Maddy had held back.

"Sinclair? Did you hear me?" O'Grady demanded.

"Yeah, boss. I don't know why cow's blood was in the driveway, but that doesn't matter right now. I just saw Jackson heading into a warehouse owned by Arvani." Noah knew now the man he'd seen was actually his partner. "I'm heading in."

"I'll send backup."

"Good idea. Matt Callahan just arrived," Noah said, noticing the dark vehicle without lights that pulled up to the curb. He could see the familiar face of Duchess, Matt's German shepherd, in the back. "We're going in. Make sure the other squads that respond come in without lights or sirens."

O'Grady snorted, then hung up. Noah slid the phone back into his pocket and glanced at Maddy. "I need you to go back to the truck to wait for us."

"Not happening." Her tone was firm.

He hoped Matt would be able to talk some sense into her. Matt and Duchess quickly joined them.

Noah quickly filled him in on the bullet he'd found and the owner of the warehouse. He finished with how he'd witnessed his partner heading inside.

Matt scowled. "What's the plan?"

"I'm going in. I'd like you and Duchess to back me up, and Maddy to wait in the car."

"His lieutenant is sending additional backup," Maddy interjected. "We can always wait for them to arrive."

The sounds of loud voices wafted from inside the warehouse. Then the sharp retort of a gunshot ripped through the air.

Noah knew there wasn't time to wait. He turned and ran toward the doorway. It wasn't locked, so he drew it open and flattened himself against the inside wall, raking his gaze over the area.

The inside of the warehouse wasn't a wide-open space the way he'd expected. It was partitioned off into separate rooms. The entryway where he stood was clear, but he could still hear the raised voices arguing heatedly. He slid along the edge of the wall, trying to pinpoint exactly where the argument was coming from.

Noah could tell by the slight click of toenails on the concrete that Matt and Duchess had come inside to join him. He hoped and prayed Maddy had returned to the truck.

Since thinking about Maddy being in danger was nothing but a distraction, he pushed it from his mind and slipped farther into the warehouse.

Matt tapped him on the shoulder and pointed to a room off to the right, indicating that was where the shouting was coming from. Noah nodded and turned in that direction.

A few steps brought him within arm's reach of the door. The arguing continued, only now he could distinguish what was being said.

"You failed to get rid of the ADA," someone said. "Why should we pay you?"

"Because I need the cash to complete the task," the other one shouted. The voice sounded an awful lot like Jackson's. "There's still time. I'm doing my best considering she has cops all over her."

"You should have taken care of her and your partner on that first night, before they left town."

Noah wondered if the latter voice belonged to Arvani. His memory of the guy who'd trained with him at the academy was faint at best. They hadn't been friends, and Noah had been focused on learning everything he needed to be the best cop he could be.

Only that hadn't worked out very well, had it? His inability to keep a partner didn't bode well for his future as a cop. At least now he understood why Jackson hadn't given him any grief about trusting Noah to have his back.

The guy himself had probably been involved with Pietro's business dealings all along. Nothing else made any sense.

Focus, he told himself harshly. He glanced at Matt, struck by a horrible sense of uncertainty. Should they wait for the rest of their backup to arrive? Or barge in?

Matt steadily held his gaze, giving the impression he had confidence in Noah's decision. Too bad he wasn't so sure he deserved it.

Noah was about to give the signal to move in when the door behind them barged open. A man entered, pulling Maddy along with him, a gun pointed at her head.

Lance Arvani. The bitter taste of failure stuck in Noah's throat, knowing that he and Matt were now outnumbered.

If Maddy was injured or worse, he knew it would be his fault.

He'd failed her once again.

Maddy hated seeing the sick expression on Noah's and Matt's faces. Her stubborn insistence on sticking around until their backup arrived had not only placed herself in danger, but Noah and Matt, as well.

She wasn't sure who had her, but the gravelly voice had been all too familiar. It was the same guy who'd assaulted her outside the courthouse the night she'd lost her memory.

"Okay, let's stay calm," Noah said, raising his hands up in the universal gesture of surrender. "You really don't want to shoot a couple of cops and an ADA, do you?"

"Release Pietro and we'll see what we can work out," the gravelly voice said.

It took every ounce of effort she had not to react to that

ridiculous demand. Even if she believed the gunman would let them all go, which she didn't, there was no way she'd allow Pietro to walk away from his crimes.

Never.

There had to be a way out of this. There just had to be!

Noah's gaze met hers for a long moment before shifting to the man holding a gun on her. In that second, she knew that Noah planned to do whatever he deemed necessary in order to save her life.

That he'd sacrifice himself to avoid having another death on his conscience.

But this mess was her fault for not obeying his directive to return to the truck, not his. And really, all she needed to do was to stall until the rest of their backup arrived. In fact, she was a bit surprised they hadn't shown up already.

Tension shimmered in the air as the gunman faced off with her brother and the man she'd grown to care about.

To love.

Maddy didn't let herself dwell on that thought; she needed to stay focused on finding a way out of the situation she'd gotten them into. The gunman held her tightly, but not so much that she couldn't move.

She'd grown up with five older brothers, each of them making it their mission to make sure she knew how to protect herself. There had to be a way to escape. Even if none of the scenarios her brothers had taught involved a man actually holding a gun to her head.

Maybe she could improvise.

"Come on, Arvani," Noah said. "Let's find a way to end this in a way that we're both happy."

The man, obviously Lance Arvani, snickered. "I don't care what you want. I'm the one holding a gun to the pretty ADA's head. You'll both do exactly what I tell you. Drop your weapons and kick them toward me, nice and easy now. Any wrong move and I'll shoot the woman."

She doubted he'd do that since they still outnumbered Arvani, at least for the moment. But she was sure the men arguing inside the room off the hall would be coming out soon. Their voices were still raised in anger, or they might have heard the commotion already.

Maddy nearly missed the hand signal Matt gave Duchess, but suddenly the dog let out a series of ferocious barks. Arvani instinctively recoiled, moving backward a step, and she took advantage of the gunman's momentary distraction to twist out of his grasp, pushing his gun up and out of the way.

"Get down," Noah roared seconds before shots filled the air.

This time she listened without question, dropping to the ground and rolling away from Arvani. Noah's aim was true; his shot hit the Chicago cop in the chest, sending him staggering backward. She wondered if he was wearing a vest, too, since he didn't go down and there was no evidence of blood. Arvani sagged against the wall, struggling to breathe.

Unfortunately the sound of Noah's gunfire brought the others running from the adjacent room. Matt stood with his legs wide and his weapon raised. "Stop! Police! Put your hands up where I can see them!"

Arvani's upper lip curled with derision and he brought his gun up, aiming at Noah. *No!* Maddy surged to her feet, intending to rush forward, hoping to disarm him when he turned and shot at her instead of Noah.

The slug hit her in the chest dead center over her heart. Despite being protected in part by the bulletproof vest, she heard a distinct crack of a broken bone. The force of the blast knocked her off her feet. She fell to the ground, pain spreading through her chest as she fought to fill her lungs with oxygen.

A red haze of pain clouded her vision and she felt completely, utterly helpless. Being shot even while wearing a vest hurt! More than she'd thought possible.

Her head jerked up as Noah fired again, this time hitting Lance Arvani in the head. The Chicago cop fell straight back like a tree hitting the forest floor.

She put a hand to her chest, still fighting the pain. Every breath was painful, a sharp stabbing sensation. Was it possible that a shot to the chest could cause a heart attack? Because that was how it felt.

Noah turned to help Matt apprehend the others. Duchess did her part, chasing after one guy who'd taken off toward the rear of the warehouse. It didn't take long for the dog to catch him, taking him down with a flying leap and then standing on top of him, her jaws open across his throat.

Matt glanced at Maddy, and she gave him a reassuring nod. He went after his partner, throwing cuffs on the wrists of the man Duchess had apprehended.

Noah was securing a short guy with bright red hair. "Jackson Dellis, you're under arrest for attempting to shoot a police officer."

The door to the warehouse burst open and more cops swarmed in, their weapons held ready. Maddy scooted over to the side of the hallway, trying to stay out of their way. Her chest ached so bad she didn't think she could stand under her own power.

"Are you all right?" Noah asked, coming over to kneel beside her, his brown eyes dark with concern.

She tried to nod, grimaced. "Hurts," she managed. Thinking about the way Noah had run after being shot in the back of his vest filled her with admiration. She couldn't do anything but lie there, struggling to breathe.

"We need paramedics," Noah said in a sharp tone.

An unexpected gunshot echoed through the room. Noah's reaction was to throw himself over her body as an added protection.

Her head hit the concrete with a loud crack.

And then there was nothing but darkness.

SEVENTEEN

What was going on? Who'd discharged their weapon? One of the cops who'd responded to the call?

Noah lifted his head in time to see Matt take out the perp who'd taken that last shot. The gunman was dressed head to toe in black, his face hidden behind a scruffy beard. The guy howled and dropped to the ground, holding his hands over his belly. He must have been hiding, because Noah had been certain they'd secured the area.

His heart thundered in his chest. That had been far too close.

The rest of the police officers who'd arrived on the scene spread out in an effort to make sure they hadn't missed anyone else.

Noah lifted himself off Maddy. "Sorry about that. Are you okay?"

Maddy didn't move and a sharp stab of fear lanced his heart.

"Maddy?" he called, trying again. Her face was pale, her eyes were closed and it was difficult for him to tell if she was breathing. Panic hit hard. "We need that ambulance! Now!"

"What's wrong?" Matt finished cuffing the perp Duchess had chased down, then came over to kneel beside him.

"I'm not sure," Noah confessed. "She was awake and talking, but now she's out cold." He placed his fingers along the side of her neck searching for a pulse, only slightly reassured when he found the weak, rapid beat.

"The ambulance just pulled up." The officer who spoke wore a nametag that identified him as Jennings.

"Tell them ADA Callahan needs attention." Noah glanced down again at Maddy's motionless face. "Maddy? Can you hear me?"

Still nothing. He took a deep breath, lowered his head and prayed.

Dear Lord, please heal Maddy's injuries and keep her safe in Your care!

"Was she shot?" Matt asked, pushing her sweatshirt out of the way and running his fingertips over the material of the vest. His hand stopped when he found the slug. "She took one right over the center of her chest. Let's get this thing off, make sure she's not bleeding."

Noah assisted in removing the Velcro straps to remove the vest. Thankfully Maddy wore a T-shirt underneath. There was no sign of blood, but he knew only too well how being hit in the vest at close range could still cause serious harm. What if somehow the bullet had managed to damage her heart or her lungs?

Two paramedics pushed their way through the crowd of cops, heading toward them. Matt rose to his feet, gesturing for them to come closer. Noah didn't let go of Maddy's hand, afraid that if he did she'd slip away.

"Hang in there, Maddy. I'm here and so is Matt. Hang in there, understand?"

She didn't respond to his running commentary, and that only worried him more. She had to be okay. She just had to!

The thought of living his life without her made his eyes

grow damp. He didn't do relationships, hadn't wanted to hurt anyone the way he'd hurt Gina, but his heart hadn't listened to his head.

He'd fallen in love with Maddy Callahan.

"There's a small lump on the back of her head," one of the paramedics said. "She may have a brain injury."

"She was hit on the head a few days ago, but that was along her right temple," Noah said with a frown.

"This one is dead center on the back of her head. She may have hit her head against the concrete."

Noah's stomach knotted and he forced himself to look at Matt. "I did this," he said in a hoarse tone. "I threw myself on top of her and must have knocked her head against the floor by accident!"

"Hey, it's okay," Matt said reassuringly. "You were only trying to help. Besides, Maddy has a pretty hard head. I'm sure she'll be fine."

Noah wanted to believe him. Guilt rose in the back of his throat, threatening to choke him, but he pushed it back and focused on the power of prayer.

He desperately needed to believe Maddy would wake up. And God was the one who could make that happen.

Muffled voices pierced the darkness. While it was tempting to shut them out, melting back into the soft velvet blackness, she couldn't shake off the sense of urgency.

With a low moan, Maddy pushed past the pain in her head and her chest and tried to open her eyes.

"Maddy?" The familiar scent of spicy aftershave helped bring the image of Noah's concerned face into focus. "You're awake!"

She winced at the volume of his tone. "Yes," she managed. "Water?"

"Right here." Noah's voice was soft and gentle now. He

slid his arm beneath her shoulder blades and held a cup to her lips. The cool water tasted amazing and she took several long sips. "Thanks."

"I'm so glad you're awake," Noah said, concern etched in his features. His appearance was ragged, dark stubble covered his cheeks and chin and his eyes were bloodshot. He looked as if he'd been awake for days. "I'll get the doctor."

"Wait," she said as understanding dawned. "I'm in the hospital? For how long?"

"It's almost noon on Thursday," Noah informed her. "You've been in since late last night."

Good to know she hadn't lost too much prep time. Well, other than what she'd already lost since Monday night when she'd left the courthouse and been assaulted. By Lance Arvani, she remembered now.

"Arvani was the one who accosted me and threatened my mother and grandmother," she said. "I recognized his voice."

"He's dead, so you don't have to worry about him any longer," Noah said. "And we've arrested Jackson Dellis, too. He's not talking yet, but I'm sure he'll break down eventually. I'd really like to know why he faked his death."

Images from the scene at the warehouse fluttered through her mind. "Maybe he tried to set you up."

Noah shrugged. "Anything's possible. I'd better get the doctor. Your family should be here soon. They took a quick break for lunch."

"You stayed," Maddy said, looking down at their joined hands. "Thank you, Noah."

"I'm sorry I caused you to hit your head again," he said, averting his gaze. "I never wanted to hurt you."

He tried to pull away, but she tightened her grip, keeping him there. "You protected me from the very beginning," she reminded him. "I owe you my life, Noah. Thank you."

"I almost killed you," he corrected.

She glared at him, even though it made her headache worse. "I'm pretty sure it was my own fault that Lance Arvani caught me and held me at gunpoint in the first place." She lifted her hand to her chest, wondering how badly she was bruised. "Just accept my gratitude, would you? Please?"

He slowly nodded. "Okay. Now can I get the doctor?"

Her fingers reflexively tightened around his. She didn't want to let him go.

Not now. Not ever. But how to explain that she felt safe only when she was with him? That he was the only man she could tolerate being close to?

The only man she wanted with her whole heart?

There was a knock at her door, then it opened, revealing a tall, thin bald man wearing a lab coat. "Good morning, Ms. Callahan. I'm Dr. Eduardo and I'm glad to see you're awake. How are you feeling?"

"Fine," she lied. The pounding behind her eyes was reminiscent of the first time she'd hit her head. But she knew the headache would fade in time. "How soon can I be discharged?"

Dr. Eduardo's eyebrows levered up. "Discharged? We'll see how you're feeling by tomorrow morning. I have a repeat CT scan scheduled for this afternoon. I want to be sure you don't have any internal bleeding in your brain. And you may be interested to know you have a cracked rib."

The cracked rib wasn't much of a surprise, but a repeat CT scan? Weird that she couldn't remember the first one. "Okay, that's fine, but if the scan is clear I'm leaving. I have a case going to trial on Monday."

Dr. Eduardo's scowl deepened. "You need to rest and relax."

"And I will," Maddy said. "After the trial."

He made a disgusted sound, then proceeded to examine her. By the time he'd finished, her family had returned from lunch. All of them.

"Oh, Maddy." Her mother's eyes were suspiciously bright as Margaret Callahan rushed over to hug her. "I'm so glad you're awake."

Her mother always smelled like chocolate-chip cookies, maybe because she was always making a new batch. Maddy kissed her cheek, then smiled at her mother and her grandmother, who came up to the other side of her bed. Nan, who loved to knit, held Marc and Kari's seven-month-old son, Max, on her hip. The boy stuck his fist in his mouth, revealing several new teeth.

"I'm glad you're both safe," Maddy said in a low tone. "The man who threatened you is dead, so there's no need to worry."

"Worry? Me?" Her mother patted her arm. "I've never worried about myself, just my children. Especially since each one of you seems to be constantly in harm's way. No more injuries, you hear me?"

"At least I don't have a bullet wound," Maddy pointed out, trying to lighten things up.

"Only because you were smart enough to be wearing a vest," Matt said drily.

Her twin, along with the rest of her brothers, crowded around. Paige and her daughter, Abby, stood next to Margaret. The baby, Max, wasn't Marc's biological son, but the way the Callahans fawned over him, you'd never know it. Both kids, Max and Abby, were well loved and welcomed with open arms.

Her mother had found a way to speed up the process of

getting the grandchildren she'd always wanted. Although Maddy knew she was literally counting the days until either Kari or Paige announced they were pregnant.

"I'm fine, really," she assured them. She looked for Noah, disappointed to see he'd stepped back, remaining near the doorway as if he didn't belong. "Thanks to Noah. He saved my life more times than I can count."

Several Callahan heads swiveled in his direction and even from here she could see him blush from the intense attention.

"Thanks, Sinclair," Matt and Mike said at the same time. They glanced at each other and snickered.

Maddy kept her gaze on Noah, silently asking him to come closer. He didn't.

Max squirmed and kicked so Nan handed him over to Marc. His wails grew louder.

"Oh, dear, we'd better get Max home for a nap," Kari said, taking her son into her arms.

"Yes, we'll need to head home, too," Paige said.

"I wouldn't mind some rest," Maddy said.

"We'll all go," her mother agreed. "We'll check back later, okay?"

"Thanks, Mom." It took several minutes for her family to file out of the room, and she couldn't help but be thankful for the silence they left behind. She loved every one of them more than anything, but the ache in her head appreciated the quiet. When she saw Noah move toward the door, she called, "Wait."

He stopped, then turned toward her. "What is it?"

"Please stay." When she raised her hand, he stepped forward to take it. "I feel safer when you're with me."

"Of course," he said without hesitation.

"Remember when you asked me if someone—a man— hurt me?" she asked.

Noah went tense instantly knowing what she meant. "Yes."

"Thankfully I escaped, but it was a close call," she admitted. "I've avoided men since the incident, except for you, Noah."

His expression softened and he bent down, gently pressing a kiss to her forehead. "I'm glad. Even though I want to break his face."

She smiled, filling her head with his woodsy scent. "He's not worth the effort. But I do have a favor to ask."

"Anything."

His quick response warmed her heart. "Will you keep me company as I continue prepping for the trial?"

"Absolutely. Although I want you to remain in the hospital overnight. No more taking chances with your health."

Tomorrow was Friday, which would leave only three days to get ready for the trial. She should continue preparing witnesses. There were several officers yet that she hadn't worked with.

The pain in her head intensified, making her realize that maybe she was about as ready as she needed to be.

"I will if you stay with me," she acquiesced.

A smile tugged at the corner of his mouth. "You have a deal."

Maddy closed her eyes and felt every ounce of tension leave her body. With Noah at her side, she could face just about anything.

The three days before the trial passed in a blur. Maddy couldn't work nonstop the way she normally did, and that only added to her frustration.

Noah displayed infinite patience, and she knew she was fortunate to have him staying close to her side while she either slept or prepared for the trial. Since Maddy's condo was still fire damaged, she and Noah moved to a motel not far from the courthouse, paid for by her boss, Jarrod Fine.

Early Monday morning, Maddy woke up feeling better than she had since the warehouse shooting. Her rib still screamed at her if she moved too quickly, or coughed or sneezed, but the pain in her head had finally receded to a tolerable level.

She dressed carefully in a red power suit and a black blouse, refusing to let Pietro know how close he'd come to achieving his goal of getting rid of her.

"Wow," Noah said as he emerged from his connecting room. His gaze held frank admiration. "You look amazing."

"So do you." Noah wore a navy blue suit, white shirt and red tie. She'd rearranged her witness list so that Noah would be first to testify. It was good for her case, plus, she thought selfishly, he'd be free to sit in the courtroom once he'd finished testifying.

For a moment she just stared at him. In the past few days she'd avoided personal conversations, forcing herself to focus on the trial. But at the moment, she couldn't think of anything but how much Noah meant to her.

She walked over to him, reaching up to straighten his tie, even though it wasn't at all crooked. "Noah, once this trial is over, I'd like to see you again."

He seemed flabbergasted by her statement. "Um, you would?"

His less than enthusiastic response wasn't reassuring; still, she soldiered on. "I'd love for you to join me for church services followed by Sunday brunch with my family."

The tension eased from his body. "Oh, sure. That sounds great. In fact, you should know that I've been praying a lot recently."

"You have?" She was touched by the return of his faith. "I'm happy to hear that."

He reached up and brushed a stray hair off her cheek. "Mostly about you, Maddy. You keep saying I've saved your life, but in reality, you've saved mine, too. More than you realize."

"Oh, Noah." She reached up and kissed him. For a moment he held her close, then he quickly let her go. She missed having his arms around her but stepped back, anxious to get to the courthouse. "We'll talk further after the trial, okay?"

"You and your deals," he lightly teased.

They pulled on their winter gear and walked outside. There was a hint of sunlight on the horizon, but the air was crisp and cold.

They were the first ones in line at the courthouse doorway. She showed her badge so the sheriff's deputy waved her through without making her go through the metal detector. Noah had to go through the process of emptying his pockets and being scanned through, but since he was a witness, he couldn't carry his weapon.

Up in Judge Dugan's courtroom, Maddy took her seat at the prosecutor's table and pulled out her notes.

This was it.

The moment she'd been waiting for. Despite losing a few of her witnesses, she still had what she believed was a solid case. In fact, the news of Lance Arvani's death had rippled through what was left of Pietro's organization and Jackson Dellis was among others who were now willing to talk in exchange for a lighter sentence.

Dellis had admitted that setting up his own murder had been an attempt to discredit Noah Sinclair and his subsequent testimony against Pietro. A plan that had, unfortunately, backfired. Maddy was sure that putting Dellis on the stand would be the final nail in Pietro's case.

Over the next ninety minutes, the courtroom filled up. Two deputies brought in Alexander Pietro, dressed in a suave pin-striped suit that was supposed to make him look professional but only reminded her of old gangster movies.

A woman dressed in a tight gold sweater dress and spiked heels entered the gallery, choosing to sit almost directly behind Pietro. Maddy frowned, wondering who she was. Pietro didn't have any family that they'd been able to find, and his former girlfriend, Rachel Graber, had been gunned down outside her safe house.

Maddy leaned toward her brother Matt. "I need to know who that woman is," she whispered.

Matt nodded, rose to his feet and subtly snapped a picture with his phone before leaving the courtroom.

Judge Dugan called the proceedings to order and once they finished with their jury selection, Maddy was allowed to call her first witness, Milwaukee police officer Noah Sinclair.

Noah did an amazing job on the stand, the way she knew he would. The jury listened intently to his testimony and one of the younger female jurors kept staring at Noah with obvious interest.

Maddy swallowed the ridiculous surge of jealousy and continued asking questions related to Alexander Pietro's arrest. By the time she finished and Pietro's lawyer had a chance to cross-examine Noah, it was clear that Pietro's defense was in trouble.

When Noah was finished, Judge Dugan excused him from the stand. Maddy looked at her notes for a minute. "The People would like to call Officer Charles Wynn to the stand," she said, turning toward the back of the courtroom.

Without warning, the woman in gold lunged at Maddy,

her long fingernails aimed directly at her face. Before Maddy could do more than take a stumbling step backward, Noah grabbed the woman around the waist and swung her away from Maddy. The woman's talon-like fingernails raked down Noah's neck, drawing blood before he managed to get her under control.

"Order," Judge Dugan shouted, banging his gavel. "Order in the courtroom!"

The bailiff and another deputy ran over to help subdue the woman, slapping cuffs on her and hauling her away. Maddy rushed toward Noah. The scratches were long but not deep. "Are you all right?"

"I'll live," Noah grunted.

Matt came in and headed toward them. "I guess I'm too late to tell you that the woman is Aleshia Tanner and she's Pietro's newest girlfriend."

Maddy let out a sigh. "I figured something like that."

"I want this courtroom cleared immediately," Judge Dugan said. "Counsel will report to my chambers in five minutes."

Maddy didn't want to leave Noah, but she didn't want to be held in contempt, either. "Matt, stay with Noah, okay? I'd like you both to wait for me. This shouldn't take long."

Judge Dugan was not at all happy with the defense and quickly made his feelings known. "The courtroom will be closed to the public moving forward," he said in a stern voice. "And I strongly suggest Mr. Pietro consider accepting a plea bargain. After that fiasco in there, the State will give him a better deal than the jury will."

"I'll see what I can do," Pietro's attorney muttered.

"Twenty-five years with the chance at parole after twenty instead of life in prison without a chance of parole," Maddy said. "The offer is only good until tomorrow morning. Trust me, the jury won't hesitate to sentence him to life without a chance at parole."

Pietro's attorney nodded again and quickly made his escape.

As she left Judge Dugan's chambers, she stopped short when she saw ADA Blake Ratcliff standing just outside the doorway, obviously coming from some other trial. Instantly nausea swirled in her stomach. "What do you want?" she asked harshly.

"Hi, Maddy." He smiled without humor. "I've been waiting for a chance to talk to you."

"Too bad. I'm not interested in talking to you." She was glad that her voice sounded strong, hoping he wouldn't notice the way her hands trembled. How was it possible that she once thought he was handsome? His fancy suit and slicked-back hair seemed ridiculous compared to Noah's rugged attractiveness.

Blake took another step toward her. She froze, then raised her chin as if daring him to come closer. Her brothers had taught her to fend for herself, and right now she couldn't think of a better person to lash out at than the man who'd tried forcing her against his desk.

Suddenly Noah came around the corner, his gaze zeroing in on Blake the way an eagle spied a fish. "Didn't you hear the lady? She said she's not interested in talking to you."

Blake scowled and turned toward Noah. She took advantage of Noah's interruption and quickly walked past, holding her head high. Once she reached Noah's side, she glanced back over her shoulder.

"Don't come near me again, Blake," she warned. "Next time, I'll press charges."

Blake's face turned beet red with anger, but when Noah

wrapped his arm around Maddy's shoulders, he shrugged, turned and walked away.

"He's the one who tried to hurt you, isn't he?" Noah asked in a low voice.

Maddy raised her gaze to his. "Yes."

Noah's brown eyes darkened with anger. "You really should press charges."

"Maybe I will." She slipped her arm around his waist and rested her head against his shoulder. "Blake isn't important, Noah, but you are."

"Me?" He sounded confused.

She shifted so that she could see his face. "I care about you, Noah. I know you said you didn't do relationships, but I hope you'll make an exception for me."

"Maddy, I—don't know what to say."

The flame of hope in her heart flickered. "Say you'll give us a chance."

Noah's answer was to pull her close and to kiss her. She clung to him, reveling in his embrace. This was what had been missing from her life. A man, a partner to share things with.

To love.

"I'll be honored to give us a chance, because I love you, Maddy," Noah whispered in her ear.

The flame brightened, filling her heart with warmth. "I love you, too."

"Oh, yippee skippy," Matt said in a sarcastic voice intended to be overheard. "Another Callahan bites the dust."

Noah let out a choked laugh but didn't loosen his grip. "I don't think being in love qualifies for biting the dust."

"Go away, Matt," Maddy said, waving a hand at him. "We don't need you after all."

"Good thing she loves you, Noah, since I distinctly remember telling you to stay away from her," Matt said.

"Knock it off already!" Maddy threw the words over her shoulder. "Three's a crowd, Matt."

"Okay, but you need to answer your phone, sis," Matt said. "Your boss is on the line. Apparently Pietro accepted your offer. The trial is officially over."

"That's great news," Noah agreed.

"Yes." Maddy rose up on her tiptoes to kiss him again. The trial was over.

But her life with Noah was just beginning.

EPILOGUE

Christmas Eve

Maddy opened the door, smiling brightly in greeting. Noah stepped over the threshold into the Callahan family home, struck anew by the plethora of Christmas decorations. The place looked amazing, and he was glad Maddy was living there while her condo was being rebuilt. Although she'd already mentioned that living downtown had lost its appeal.

He hoped that meant she'd be willing to consider living somewhere more modest, like the small home he'd purchased last summer. It wasn't nearly as grand as her mother's home, but it was a start.

"Noah!" Maddy greeted him with an exuberant hug and kiss. He held her for an extra minute, savoring the cinnamon scent that clung to her skin. "You're late," she accused softly.

He wasn't about to explain why he'd run late, at least not yet. "Everyone else is here?" He swallowed hard. "Your entire family?"

"Yep. Come on. Dinner won't be ready for a while yet, so everyone is gathered in the family room." She took his hand and tugged him toward the sound of voices inter-mixed with laughter.

The idea of giving Maddy his gift tonight had seemed like a good idea at the time, but now he was having second thoughts. The family room was chock-full of Calla-hans. He knew them all by name, of course, and in birth order, too. Marc was the eldest, married to Kari, then came Miles, who was married to Paige. Then there was Mitch, Michael, Matthew and finally Maddy.

The woman he loved with his whole heart.

Maddy took a seat on the corner of the sofa and indi-cated he should sit beside her.

Instead he walked around until he was directly in front of her and dropped to one knee.

The room instantly went silent; even the kids didn't make a sound. He wasn't sure if that was a good thing or not, but he'd come this far. It was too late to turn back now.

"Maddy? Will you please marry me?" He took the ring box out of his pocket, opened the lid and held it out to her. Picking up the diamond ring had been the reason he'd run a little late.

"Oh, Noah! Yes! Of course I'll marry you!" She didn't bother looking at the ring but launched herself into his arms.

"Yay!"

"It's about time!"

"Wow, that was quick!"

"Aw, isn't that sweet?"

The comments from her family were like white noise in the background. Nothing mattered at that moment except Maddy.

She'd said yes!

"Is there gonna be a baby in her tummy, too?" a young voice asked. "Like Auntie Kari?"

The adults laughed at Abby's innocent question. Noah hoped his face wasn't too red.

"Wait, what?" Maddy pulled out of his arms, turning to look at her eldest brother. "You're having a baby?"

"We are," Marc confirmed. "In about four and a half months, so please plan to have your wedding before Kari delivers."

"Yeah, because, um, so are we," Paige spoke up, blushing as Miles placed his hand over her still flat belly. "Having a baby, I mean. About the same time as Marc and Kari."

The room broke out into laughter and applause with a few low male groans from the brothers who were still single. Noah didn't mind fitting in his wedding to Maddy before or after babies. This was the family he'd dreamed of.

With Maddy at his side, he was exactly where he belonged.

* * * * *

Dear Reader,

Christmas Amnesia is the third book in my Callahan Confidential miniseries. Thanks to all of you who wrote to me letting me know how much you're enjoying the Callahans. This book revolves around Assistant District Attorney Madison "Maddy" Callahan.

When Maddy is assaulted outside the courthouse, she loses her memory, a catastrophe since she's preparing for the biggest trial of her career. Office Noah Sinclair arrives at the hospital in time to save her life, and while he certainly knows Maddy, she doesn't remember him. As Maddy tries to remember and flees the gunman chasing after her, she soon realizes Noah is the only man she can trust, with her life and with her heart.

I hope you enjoy Noah and Maddy's story. I'm also hard at work on the next book in the Callahan Confidential Series. I love hearing from my readers. If you're interested in contacting me or signing up for my newsletter, please visit my website at www.laurascottbooks.com. I'm also on Facebook at Laura Scott Books Author and on Twitter @Laurascottbooks.

Yours in faith,
Laura Scott

COMING NEXT MONTH FROM
Love Inspired® Suspense

Available November 7, 2017

Get 2 Free Books,

Plus 2 Free Gifts—

just for trying the Reader Service!

*Texas Ranger Colt Blackthorn has only one goal—catch
Adriana Garcia, sister of a notorious crime boss and suspected
killer of Colt's best friend. Finally, just before Christmas, he
has his eyes on the target...or does he? A case of mistaken
identity has put Danielle Segovia in harm's way, so it's up to
Colt to make things right by keeping her safe.*

Read on for a sneak preview of
Jodie Bailey's CHRISTMAS DOUBLE CROSS,
the exciting beginning of the new miniseries
TEXAS RANGER HOLIDAYS,
available November 2017 from Love Inspired Suspense!

"Ms. Segovia." Colt leaned forward, his dark eyes serious. "We
have a problem."

Adrenaline jolted against Danielle's chest and throbbed in
the bruise on her cheek. "Whatever you think I did, I didn't. I've
never—"

"It's not you." Glancing down at his cell phone and flicking
through a couple of screens, he said, "Do you know who Rio
Garcia is?"

Danielle's head jerked back in shock. Rio Garcia was the
leader of a notorious drug cartel. Everyone knew that name. He
was known for his calculated cunning and his murderous rages,
for his ability to slip away from the authorities even when they
believed they had him cornered.

"I don't have any connection to him."

"But the men who tried to kidnap you tonight may."

Danielle's muscles went weak. If she wasn't already lying
down, she'd melt to the floor. "Why?"

Colt didn't answer the question immediately. He stared at his cell phone for what felt like an eternity, then studied Danielle's face before passing the device to her without a word.

Hand trembling, Danielle took the phone.

At first glance, the woman staring back up at her could be her twin sister. They had the same hair, the same eyes, but the other woman had a small scar next to her ear. Still, the resemblance was enough to make her feel she'd fallen out of reality into a very bad horror movie. "Who is this?"

Colt studied her as though her reaction to what he was about to say was of vital importance. "Her name is Adriana Garcia."

Garcia. Heart pounding, Danielle stared at the woman. "She looks like me."

Holding out his hand, Colt took the phone and pocketed it. "She's Rio Garcia's sister. She's wanted by both sides of the law for multiple reasons, and both sides will do whatever it takes to get to her first."

"Why is he having to search for his own sister?" She couldn't fathom that sort of distance between siblings. "I don't understand."

"The most I can tell you is that she stole something from him, and he wants it back." He laid a hand on hers. "We had intel that suggested you were her, but as you know, that intel was bad. The problem is, we believe Rio Garcia received the same intel, and that those were his men who came after you."

Danielle shook her head. She wasn't hearing this. It couldn't be true.

Because if a killer like Rio Garcia believed she was the person he wanted, he would stop at nothing to drag her to him.

Don't miss
CHRISTMAS DOUBLE CROSS by Jodie Bailey,
available November 2017 wherever
Love Inspired® Suspense books and ebooks are sold.

www.LoveInspired.com

Inspirational Romance to
Warm Your Heart and Soul

Join our social communities to connect
with other readers who share your love!

Sign up for the Love Inspired newsletter
at **www.LoveInspired.com** to be the
first to find out about upcoming titles,
special promotions and exclusive content.

CONNECT WITH US AT:

Harlequin.com/Community

 Facebook.com/LoveInspiredBooks

 Twitter.com/LoveInspiredBks

LISOCIAL2017

SPECIAL EXCERPT FROM

When Erica Lindholm and her twin babies show up at his family farm just before Christmas, Jason Stephanidis can tell she's hiding something. But how can he refuse the young mother, a friend of his sister's, a place to stay during the holidays? He never counted on wanting Erica and the boys to be a more permanent part of his life...

Read on for a sneak peek of
SECRET CHRISTMAS TWINS
*by **Lee Tobin McClain**,*
*part of the **CHRISTMAS TWINS** miniseries.*

Once both twins were bundled, snug between Papa and Erica, Jason sent the horses trotting forward. The sun was up now, making millions of diamonds on the snow that stretched across the hills far into the distance. He smelled pine, a sharp, resin-laden sweetness.

When he picked up the pace, the sleigh bells jingled.

"Real sleigh bells!" Erica said, and then, as they approached the white covered bridge decorated with a simple wreath for Christmas, she gasped. "This is the most beautiful place I've ever seen."

Jason glanced back, unable to resist watching her fall in love with his home.

Papa was smiling for the first time since he'd learned of Kimmie's death. And as they crossed the bridge and trotted toward the church, converging with other horse-drawn sleighs, Jason felt a sense of rightness.

LIEXP1017

Mikey started babbling to Teddy, accompanied by gestures and much repetition of his new word. Teddy tilted his head to one side and burst forth with his own stream of nonsense syllables, seeming to ask a question, batting Mikey on the arm. Mikey waved toward the horses and jabbered some more, as if he were explaining something important.

They were such personalities, even as little as they were. Jason couldn't help smiling as he watched them interact.

Once Papa had the reins set and the horses tied up, Jason jumped out of the sleigh, and then turned to help Erica down. She handed him a twin. "Can you hold Mikey?"

He caught a whiff of baby powder and pulled the little one tight against his shoulder. Then he reached out to help Erica, and she took his hand to climb down, Teddy on her hip.

When he held her hand, something electric seemed to travel right to his heart. Involuntarily he squeezed and held on.

She drew in a sharp breath as she looked at him, some mixture of puzzlement and awareness in her eyes.

What was Erica's secret?

And wasn't it curious that, after all these years, there were twins in the farmhouse again?

Don't miss
SECRET CHRISTMAS TWINS
by Lee Tobin McClain, available November 2017
wherever Love Inspired® books and ebooks are sold.

www.LoveInspired.com

LIEXP1017